REVENGE AT CAMP TEPEKI

megan Spengler

may 5, 2014

REVENGE AT CAMP TEPEKI

Megan Spengler

TATE PUBLISHING
AND ENTERPRISES, LLC

Revenge at Camp Tepeki
Copyright © 2014 by Megan Spengler. All rights reserved.

No part of this publication may be reproduced, stored in a retrieval system or transmitted in any way by any means, electronic, mechanical, photocopy, recording or otherwise without the prior permission of the author except as provided by USA copyright law.

This novel is a work of fiction. Names, descriptions, entities, and incidents included in the story are products of the author's imagination. Any resemblance to actual persons, events, and entities is entirely coincidental.

The opinions expressed by the author are not necessarily those of Tate Publishing, LLC.

Published by Tate Publishing & Enterprises, LLC
127 E. Trade Center Terrace | Mustang, Oklahoma 73064 USA
1.888.361.9473 | www.tatepublishing.com

Tate Publishing is committed to excellence in the publishing industry. The company reflects the philosophy established by the founders, based on Psalm 68:11,
"The Lord gave the word and great was the company of those who published it."

Book design copyright © 2014 by Tate Publishing, LLC. All rights reserved.
Cover design by Joel Uber
Interior design by Jimmy Sevilleno

Published in the United States of America

ISBN: 978-1-63063-217-5
1. Fiction / Mystery & Detective / General
2. Fiction / Thrillers / General
13.12.13

To Toby, I love your creativity and joy for life. Without you, none of this is possible! Thanks for the lyrics to Camp Tepeki's song in the space of five minutes! I love you!

To the Clausing and Spengler clans, I have the best family in the world!

To Jason and Andrea, the two of you have been such an encouragement to me. It was not coincidence that God hooked us up when he did!

To Blair, thanks for tearing my story up! It needed your expertise!

To Mom, Suzanne, Pam, and Joanne, thanks for editing! You guys rock!

To Sage, thanks for helping me name Kacie. It was a perfect fit!

To Denton, thanks for harassing me to get that sloppy copy done!

To my Widewater friends, thanks for making my camp counselor experience so memorable!

To my ONU girls, thanks for all your support and encouragement! I'm blessed to call you friends!

To Tate Publishing, thanks for everything!

To my readers, thanks for all your wonderful comments and for asking when the second one was coming!

And most importantly, to my God, you have blessed me exceedingly abundantly more than I could ever have imagined. Thank you!

PRETTY IN PINK

NOAH! I WANTED to scream, stomp my feet, and throw something. Instead, I was stuck standing between my parents, watching the creep of all creeps. Being polite was taking every ounce of strength I possessed. I didn't want to be at this lousy camp anyway, and now, since Noah was here, I was most definitely not staying—a point I shared with my parents as soon as Noah and his family were no longer within hearing distance.

"You're staying, Abby," Mom said. She fanned her face with the camp brochure. Her graying bangs fluttered with the faint breeze the fan produced.

I crossed my arms and refused to move ahead in line. "No. I'm not spending two weeks in the woods with *him*."

Dad grabbed my arm and tugged me forward, sending apologetic glances to the people in line behind us. "Yes, you are. We already paid, and the money is nonrefundable."

"Then maybe you should have listened to me when I said I didn't want to come." I glared at them. I swear I had the densest parents in the history of mankind. It's not like I hadn't told them a million times that I had no interest in going to church camp. What did they need, a neon sign?

Mom paused in her frantic fanning and rolled her eyes. "You were driving me crazy with your channel surfing. This is the perfect solution to your boredom."

"If I annoy you so much, then why don't you ship me off to boarding school? It'd be better than this place, and I'd be out of your way for good." I was so jealous of my best friend Claire right now. Her parents had taken her to Italy for the summer as a reward for getting straight As. I couldn't even imagine a summer without her, let alone two weeks at a camp with Noah.

When I couldn't go to the Winter Dance and then Noah...Well, anyway, Claire skipped the dance to hang out with me. Without her, the last months of school wouldn't have been survivable.

I'd been invited to go to Italy with her, but instead, my parents were dumping me at a stupid camp with no air-conditioning. First no Winter Dance. Now no Italy. Life is so not fair.

Mom sighed. "Don't be so dramatic. You're staying and that's final." She had this fake smile on her face. Mom always had that smile when she was annoyed with me and didn't want anyone but me to know.

I wanted to stick my tongue out at her, but she would just ground me after camp was over. "Well, just so you know, I'm going to hate it here, and I'm going to be miserable the whole time. Especially since that kid is here." I couldn't even say his name.

Dad tweaked my nose and waggled his bushy eyebrows. "Well, try and have a little fun."

"I'll probably die from dehydration before lights out," I grumbled. "Then you'll be rid of me forever." I wiped a bead of sweat off my forehead. "Try to cry at my funeral. I know it'll be hard since you think I'm such a pest."

Mom swatted me with her fan. "Abigail Renee, that is quite enough."

I frowned at her. Mom's use of my middle name meant I needed to knock it off, but that didn't mean I couldn't express my anger through my facial expression.

Mom and Dad got me registered, pretending to be oblivious to my glares and monotone answers to the way-too-happy lady behind the desk. After registering, we headed to the unair-conditioned cabin I'd been assigned to. Mom and Dad pointed out the arts and crafts building, the rec hall, and the sign for canoeing. If they thought it was going to be so much fun, they should have signed up for camp. I would gladly have stayed at home by myself. Once we got to the decrepit cabin, Dad set my suitcase on the wood-chipped trail in front of the porch.

"Have a good time." Dad leaned down to kiss my sweaty cheek. "We'll see you in two weeks."

Mom was blinking back tears. Now, it was my turn to roll my eyes. I had thought she wanted to get rid of me.

"We'll see you soon." She enveloped me in a big bear hug, which I didn't return.

I said a short good-bye and turned my back on them. They weren't going to get overly affectionate farewells from me when they were abandoning me in the middle of nowhere. I studied the place I was supposed to call home for the longest two weeks of my life.

The log cabin had a couple of dirty windows framed by forest green shutters in the front. You couldn't even see through the windows; they were so filthy. The two rickety steps up to the sagging porch must have been safe, but they didn't look it. The screen door had several rips in it. Mom and Dad had paid money to send me here? I sighed, climbed the steps, and went inside.

I let the door slam shut behind me and took in my surroundings. Metal bunk beds lined both walls of the cabin. Several girls were rolling out sleeping bags and chattering with each other. A woman, I assumed to be the counselor, was chatting with a couple of parents. I had no idea what bunk to pick.

Suddenly, a girl with dark brown curly hair jumped up from the bunk in front of me. She was dressed entirely in pink—shoes, glittery headband, and all. "Hi! My name's Kacie. Kacie Kohl. What's yours?"

"Abby."

Kacie grinned, and I was almost blinded by her sparkling white teeth. "I'm so excited to be here! I love hiking and learning new things, don't you?"

I shrugged. "Sure. I guess."

"I'm hoping we see all kinds of things, except maybe a bear. That would be really scary," she said, her brown eyes sparkling.

"Are there bears around here?"

"Yup. Do you think you would run away if you saw one or would you freeze?" Kacie asked, bouncing from one foot to the other. "I think I would freeze and then maybe scream."

"Well, uh, it sounds like you've really been thinking about this." I wrinkled my forehead. "I guess I would probably run away or maybe try to scare it away."

"Just don't pet any cubs if you see them."

Was she for real? I was pretty sure petting wild bear cubs wasn't on the top of anyone's to-do list. Kacie looked pretty serious, so I replied with a safe comment. "Thanks for the advice. I'll do my best to remember that."

She leaned toward me and whispered, "I'm hoping we have some cute boys in our group. That would make this summer the best ever!"

Great. Another boy-crazy girl.

"We're in the Beaver group," Kacie said. "We get to meet the boys in our group for sure tomorrow. I can't wait!" She grabbed my hand. "Since you're my first friend here, we have to make a pact."

A pact? Were we third-graders? "Umm...Okay."

"So if I see a cute boy first, you have to promise not to like him, and if you see a cute boy first, I promise not to like him. Deal?"

I found myself respecting Kacie a little. This was not a dumb girl. Claire would be impressed by Kacie's quick move to make sure I didn't steal her crush. Just before I shook her hand in agreement, a vision of Noah passed through my head. What if he was in our group? Then reality hit. It wouldn't matter at all if he was in our group. He'd already made it quite clear he was no longer into me. Besides, there was only a slim chance he'd be in our group. There were like a hundred kids here. Kacie would probably never even meet him. So, I shook her hand. "Deal."

She squeezed my hand before letting go. "I just know we're going to be the best of friends!"

I almost laughed. Of course we were. I'd just agreed not to steal her camp boyfriend.

Kacie showed me the bunk she had picked out. Her bubblegum pink sleeping bag was spread out over the bottom bunk. I tossed my plain old navy blue sleeping bag on the top bunk. My suitcase went underneath the bottom bunk right next to Kacie's and just like that, we were bunk mates. I wasn't sure I even liked Kacie, but at least I wouldn't be spending the next two weeks alone.

Before I knew it, we'd eaten a gross dinner of tuna fish casserole at the dining hall and were at the campfire. We were forced to wear these stupid beaver pins with our names on them so everyone would know which group we were in. Beavers were lame, and the pins were even lamer. They'd given the beavers googly eyes, goofy bucked teeth, and a red bow on the top of their heads. The Mosquito group would have been better. Their pins were cool, not kiddish.

Kacie pinched my arm just as I'd finished attaching my pin to my shirt. "Oh my gosh! I just saw the cutest boy! Look!"

I rubbed my arm. When I turned to look, I just knew she was talking about the boy making his way down the steps. His blondish-brown hair was slightly tousled, and a dimple appeared as he smiled at the boy he was with. He was cute all right. Too bad it was the one person I didn't want Kacie to meet—Noah. Jerk or not, I did not want her crushing on him. I was just about to tell Kacie I knew Noah from school, and we'd sort of had a thing when she poked my arm.

"Remember our pact. I saw him first!"

No, actually, I had; she just didn't know it yet. I opened my mouth to explain, but she poked me again; this time, in the ribs. Geez! I massaged my side.

"Maybe you can meet up with his friend. He's cute too," Kacie suggested, although I don't how she knew that since she was still staring at Noah.

I didn't even have to check out the friend to know he wouldn't compare to Noah, so instead, I looked at Kacie, really looked at her, and I knew she might be someone Noah would like. She was my height with beautiful curly hair, long lashes, and sweet brown eyes. Kacie was pretty. A little weird, but really pretty. I tried to explain again. "Kacie—"

"I'm going to meet him," Kacie said. She stood up and glanced back at me. "Coming?"

I didn't want her to meet Noah, but I didn't want to talk to him either, so I made a decision I hoped I wouldn't regret. "I think I'll stay here and save our seats." How was I going to be able to tell her about Noah now?

She gave me a wide grin. "Great idea! I'll get the scoop on his friend for you!"

I squirmed on the wood bench. "Maybe you should just wait to see if they're in our group tomorrow."

Kacie shook her head, her curls bouncing. "No way am I going to let some other girl meet him before I do." She walked over to him.

I resisted the urge to sneak peeks at them. What were they talking about? Did he like her? Did she mention me? I wanted to pull my hair out. After what seemed like forever, Kacie returned. Her face looked exactly like my brother Kent's when he had snagged the last chocolate chip cookie on the plate.

"So, what'd you find out?" I asked, picking at the cuticle of my middle finger.

Kacie's eyes twinkled, and she giggled. "Neither of them have girlfriends. Gosh, Noah is even cuter up close! He's so nice."

I raised my eyebrows at that. "I bet."

"His friend's name is Tyler. He's cute too. And tall," Kacie said. She brushed her hair away from her face. "The best part is they're in the Beaver group! They both had beaver pins on!"

I wanted to groan. Perfect. Could this camp get any worse? It felt like God hated me. Out of a hundred kids, Noah would be in the same group as me, and, if that wasn't bad enough, God would make sure I had a front row seat to watch Kacie flirting with him. I'd rather pour bleach in my eyes, but it was way too late to try to explain things to her now. I doubted she would even believe me.

One of the female camp counselors stood up, rescuing me from my dark thoughts. She wore a visor that matched her tan camp shirt and had a perky smile on her face. "My name is Amy, and I want to welcome you to Camp Tepeki. I hope you've had fun today, meeting your new friends. If there is anything you need, please talk with me, to your counselor, or to any one of the counselors you see here. Now, let's get our first campfire started!"

A male counselor, also wearing a tan camp shirt, began talking next. "No camp experience is complete without singing silly songs and performing equally silly skits. After we sing our official camp song, Denton will teach you some of our camp's most famous silly songs." He began strumming his guitar.

I rolled my eyes. The official camp song was ridiculous. A copy of the lyrics was on the pamphlet. My dad thought it was hilarious and sang it like three times while he was filling out the registration form. Kacie apparently did not think the song was ridiculous or hilarious. She was singing with such seriousness that you'd think it was the national anthem.

> Every day I wake up
> And jump out of bed
> I say a little prayer
> And I give God praise
> Because here at Tepeki
> We're just a little freaky
> We don't eat bugs

We've got cooks in the kitchen
The Lord is my Savior
And that's who I love
I do a cannonball
And give my all
Because here at Tepeki
We're just a little freaky
Camp Tepeki
Ba boom ba boom ba boom
Camp Tepeki
Ba boom ba boom ba boom
Camp Tepeki
Camp Tepeki!

After the song, a tall, stocky counselor wearing wire-framed glasses, who I assumed was Denton, took the microphone. These silly songs were going to be totally lame, guaranteed.

In a clear baritone, Denton started singing about a purple porcupine. Kacie giggled beside me, but I rested my head on my hands wishing I were in Italy.

I felt a tap on my shoulder and turned around. Kacie did too. Behind us was a boy whose feet didn't quite touch the ground. He was seriously short.

He leaned forward. "Want to hear a scary story? It's true."

I weighed my options—listen to more purple porcupine songs or hear a potentially good scary story. A quick glance at Esther, my counselor, showed she was absorbed in the singing, so I flipped around on my bench to face the boy, and Kacie followed my lead.

"I'm Dylan." He stuck his hand out.

I was surprised by how deep his voice was. I took his hand. "Abby."

Kacie introduced herself.

"Tell us your scary story," I said.

Dylan took a deep breath and began his tale. "Five years ago, Camp Tepeki welcomed camper Eddy Jones. He was a very outgoing kid. By the first campfire, he'd already made a ton of friends, and all the girls wanted to meet him. He was a star athlete, smart, and a talented guitar player. He had it all. One day, Eddy and his special girl, Violet, decided to canoe during their free time. Violet returned, but Eddy did not. It grew dark and still there was no sign of Eddy. A search was organized."

Kacie shivered next to me. "I'll have nightmares tonight for sure!"

"The night was clear, and a full moon was out, so the search party felt they would be able to find Eddy and bring him safely back. The rescuers searched the woods all night and most of the morning, but they found no trace of Eddy." Dylan paused. "So the rescue team found the best divers in the area to search the pond. By now, everyone feared the worst. Divers searched the pond for hours, finding nothing."

I was getting into the story, not even hearing the silly songs in the background.

"The authorities began to suspect Violet of foul play. She was brought in for questioning. Violet said they had paddled out to the middle of the pond when Eddy confessed he had a girlfriend back home. Heartbroken, Violet demanded that Eddy take her back to shore. He tried to convince her he was planning on breaking up with his girlfriend, but Violet didn't believe him. After several minutes of arguing, Eddy paddled Violet back to shore."

Kacie sighed. "Poor Violet."

"Well, Violet had to figure out sometime that boys are jerks," I said matter-of-factly, tucking a strand of hair behind my ear.

Kacie stared at me.

Dylan continued with his story, "Violet claimed she had climbed out of the canoe and stomped off, leaving Eddy to get out of the canoe on his own. She swore that when she left him, he was yelling at her to come back. She marched back to camp and fifteen minutes later, when Eddy had not come up the path, she went back down to make sure he was okay. She said the canoe was floating upside down in the middle of the pond with no sign of Eddy. She immediately reported him missing."

"Violet said the camp director hadn't taken her seriously until Eddy hadn't shown up by dinner time, and two days later, he was still missing. The police received a tip from Eddy's twin brother that Eddy's girlfriend, Darcy, was in the area, and she might know something about Eddy's disappearance. It was discovered Darcy was living with her aunt for the summer, and her aunt's house was located just a few miles away from the camp."

"Darcy claimed she had not seen Eddy since he had left for camp and knew nothing about Violet. She said Eddy's brother, Davy, hated her and would do anything to get her in trouble. However, when police searched Darcy's room, they found the red jacket Eddy had been wearing when he was reported missing. Darcy said she had no idea where the jacket came from. While the police did not believe her story, they had no other evidence to support she had anything to do with Eddy's disappearance."

Kacie's eyes were wide. She was buying this story, and I had to admit I was too.

"To this day, no other trace of Eddy has ever been found. Did Violet, Davy, or Darcy have something to do with Eddy's disappearance? We may never know. But we do know Eddy might be out there somewhere. Maybe still in these woods. Some campers down at the pond have claimed to hear a guitar playing, but they couldn't find the source of the music."

Denton's guitar switched from a rowdy song to a haunting melody. Kacie jumped and gave a little screech.

I snuggled into my sweatshirt. "That was one spooky story, Dylan."

Dylan grinned.

I turned around and shivered again. That was way better than singing along to silly songs. Way better.

STINKY

Afterbreakfast the next morning, Kacie was still talking about Eddy Jones. "That story was so scary! What do you think happened to Eddy?" She stood in front of me bouncing from one foot to the other in her pink tennis shoes.

"I don't know, Kace." I was struggling to get my shoes on quickly. Esther was going to be leading us to our first activity in seconds.

"How did he know all that stuff? I mean none of the counselors said anything."

I finished tying my shoes and stood up. "No one here is going to say anything about a lost camper or no parent would leave their kids here." I tapped my finger on my nose. "We'll have to track Dylan down."

Kacie's face brightened. "That's a fabulous idea! We can figure out how he knows about Eddy."

Esther clapped her hands. "Line up, ladies! The boys are probably waiting for us."

Kacie and I quickly got in line.

Our male counselor, Chad, was already at the nature trail, waiting with the boys. He was a skinny guy with a goofy-looking goatee. He was wearing khaki shorts and a very wrinkled, blue, plaid, button-up shirt.

"Ladies, you're going to need these. You'll have a chance to fill them up again later." He handed Kacie and me neon-green water bottles and then moved on to the two girls standing next to us.

The water bottle had an attachment on it, so I strung it through the belt loop on my jean shorts. At least I wouldn't have to hold the thing all day.

"Oh! That's what that's for!" one of my bunkmates, Lisa, said. "I've been trying to figure that out." She quickly attached her water bottle to her navy striped shorts.

I smiled. "Glad I could help." I looked around to see where Kacie had disappeared to and found her chatting with Noah and Tyler. My heart sank just like my stomach does when I ride on an elevator. Great. This really was going to be the longest two weeks of my life.

Just then, Chad whistled to get everyone's attention. "Everyone should have gotten a water bottle. If you were missed, please let me know now." He paused so anyone could speak up, but no one did. "Okay. Today we're going to go on a nature walk. We'll stop for lunch and make a few other quick stops to fill up our water bottles. I'm going to ask you to try to be quiet so we don't scare any animals away. Pay attention as we'll be pointing out the different forms of wildlife and plants we find."

"Hopefully, we'll see some pretty cool things." Esther smiled. She was absolutely beautiful. Her Asian skin was glowing, and she had long, shiny, black hair. She was wearing a short, black, comfy looking skirt with a tee shirt. "Is everyone ready?"

There were lots of nods and some yawns. Minus Kacie, it was too early in the morning for anyone to be excited about anything.

"In that case, let's go!" Chad's voice made it seem like we were off on a cool African safari rather than hiking down a narrow dirt trail into an ordinary woods. He bounded down the path.

Kacie made sure she was at the front of the pack. "Come on, Abby! We don't want to miss anything!"

What could we possibly miss? At least she wasn't hanging with Noah anymore. I dragged myself to the front.

I walked down the path with Kacie, while Chad pointed out birds I'd seen a million times at home, such as robins, cardinals, and sparrows. It wasn't super interesting, but it was nice to be outside, a small breeze ruffling my hair and birds chirping. I had to admit it was much better than vegging on the couch all day watching TV. Not that I would ever tell my parents that.

Chad stopped so suddenly Kacie almost ran into him. "Quick! Gather around!" Chad whispered excitedly. He motioned with his arms, wafting a faint woodsy smell. He might not know how to iron a shirt, but he at least wore deodorant.

I tried to figure out what we were supposed to be excited about, but all I could see was a dead tree.

Fascinating. But then, a slight movement caught my eye. Gripping the tree was a slender black lizard with yellowy silver stripes and a blue tail. Kacie took a step back, but I took a step forward. Cool.

After everyone had gathered around the front of the dead tree, Chad told us about the lizard. "This is a five-lined skink. This one looks to be fairly young because of its tail and its size. When five-lined skinks are born, they all have blue tails, but when the males get older, their tails turn brown. They eat all kinds of insects and sometimes, other lizards. This one is probably looking for his breakfast."

A few minutes later, everyone had gotten a good look at the skink, and we moved on. The boys were exclaiming how cool the skink was, and all of the girls, except me, were talking about how gross and slimy it looked. I didn't care if that was the only thing we saw on this nature hike. That skink was awesome!

Before we took a break for lunch, we saw a Fowler's toad (only exciting because it had lots of warts), a flying squirrel, and some rabbits. We heard the call of a red-eyed vireo. It sounded really pretty, but we couldn't find it even though we searched the trees for several minutes.

Lunch was a plain old ham sandwich with chips, but after all the walking, it looked pretty yummy. Kacie wanted to sit with the boys, next to Noah and Tyler, but I convinced her to sit at a shaded picnic table with the other girls. She agreed reluctantly.

I had just swallowed the last bite of my sandwich when Chad told us it was time to go. He said we would still look for animals, but he would also be pointing out some native plants. We started back down the trail and Chad pointed out a plant right away—a yellow wood sorrel. It had pretty yellow flowers and leaves shaped like shamrocks.

"These are very common around here," Chad said. "If you ever get lost in the woods, you can eat them. They can be chewed raw or cooked. Native Americans used the wood sorrel for other things too, such as soothing a sore throat or alleviating thirst, so remember the wood sorrel."

We moved on, and Chad pointed out other plants like violets and wintergreen, but the wood sorrel stuck in my mind. I wondered if it soothed broken hearts too.

As we gathered around to learn about another plant whose name I didn't hear, I smelled something disgusting.

I elbowed Kacie. "Do you smell that?"

She wrinkled her nose and nodded. "What is it?"

Then I felt soft, tiny movements in my hair. The sounds of muffled giggling came from behind me. My heart began to pound. "Kacie, what is in my hair?"

Kacie looked and screamed.

I took a deep breath and tried not to panic.

We had Chad and Esther's attention instantly. Noah and Tyler were bent over, laughing hysterically. It figured they would have something to do with this.

"We'll get them out, hon. Just stand still." Esther gently combed her fingers through my hair.

After a couple of minutes of feeling fingers brushing through my hair, I heard Chad say, "Got them. Seven stinkbugs."

That explained the smell. I turned to glare at Noah. I opened my mouth to yell at him, but Chad beat me to the punch. "Boys. I don't suppose you know anything about this?"

Noah shrugged his shoulders, not able to talk because he was still trying to contain his laughter.

"Apologize to Abby," Esther said, hands on her hips.

"Sorry," they said, not looking very sorry with those huge grins on their faces.

Chad smiled. "Well, since we have these lovely specimens here, let's talk about stinkbugs."

Seriously? He was seriously going to use the bugs that were crawling around in my hair as an educational opportunity? Boys have no clue about anything.

"I'd guess most of you know what stinkbugs are, but did you know that some cultures eat them?" Chad said, completely oblivious to my annoyance.

"Eww," Kacie said. "Who would eat stinkbugs?" She made gagging noises.

"Different places eat the stinkbugs in different ways. They can be eaten raw, fried, or mixed into salsa, so make sure you check the label on your salsa for stinkbugs!" Chad said. He gently brushed the stinkbugs off the palm of his hand onto the ground. The brown, flat bugs slowly made their way into the trees. "Let's keep going. We need to get cleaned up before dinner!"

"Especially Abby! Her hair stinks!" Tyler pinched his nose shut.

"I can't smell a thing," Kacie said. "Come on, Abby." She linked her arm through mine and started walking.

I felt a glimmer of affection at her support. Just a glimmer though. Somehow, I knew that even though Noah had just pulled a gross prank on me, it wouldn't deter her from trying to gain his attention.

We hurried to our cabin so I could take a shower. My hair really did stink despite Kacie saying it didn't. I barely made it in time to go to supper with my cabinmates. Not that it mattered. They were nice, but I didn't really fit in with any of them. Kacie was the best one, but she sure wasn't Claire.

Conversation swirled around me while I thought of ways to get back at Noah. I knew he was the real mastermind of the prank.

"I'm so excited!" Lisa said. "I heard the counselors talking, and I think we're making s'mores tonight! I love s'mores!"

I perked up. Sticky marshmallow and melted chocolate...I had an idea, and it just might work. Noah had better watch his back.

Once we got to the campfire, we were allowed to sit with whoever we wanted. Kacie wanted to sit with Noah and Tyler, and I needed to sit close to them in order for my plan to work, so I didn't argue.

"I see them! They're by that humongous tree!" Kacie clapped her hands like this was the greatest thing in the world. "Hurry! Let's go make our s'mores before someone else sits next to them." Her white smile flashed even in the dark. We definitely didn't need a flashlight.

Jealousy flashed through me at the thought of Kacie and Noah all cozy on a bench together, but I agreed. My plan for Noah would make up for all of that. Kacie and I took marshmallows from one of the counselors and crouched by the fire to roast them. Actually, Kacie didn't roast hers. She caught hers on fire purposely, so it was blacker than black. Mine was perfectly golden brown. I turned my stick around to admire it. Too bad I wasn't going to get to eat it. We took our marshmallows to the supply table to put our s'mores together.

"Abby, don't you want another cracker?" Kacie asked. She was very carefully putting the top cracker on. In fact, she was concentrating so hard that the tip of her tongue was sticking out.

"Uh, no. I'm a one-cracker kind of girl," I said. Normally I would use two crackers, but if I used two crackers tonight, my plan wouldn't work.

After watching Kacie squish her cracker on perfectly, I asked if she was ready to go. She nodded.

I grinned when I saw just what I wanted to see. Noah was sitting on the end of the log bench, talking with Tyler, and not paying attention to us at all. As soon as we were close enough, I put my plan into action. I pretended to trip, and it was the acting performance of the summer. I flailed my arms, pretending to be trying to catch myself, and my marshmallow ended up smashed on the back of Noah's head, just as I had planned.

"Oh my gosh, Noah!" I said. "I must have tripped over a stick or something!"

The glare Noah sent me was priceless. "I doubt it," he said, touching the back of his head and then quickly pulling his fingers away from the sticky mess. "You did this on purpose."

Kacie sent Noah a confused look. "She tripped, Noah. You saw her."

"Dude! You have marshmallow everywhere!" Tyler guffawed, slapping his knee.

"Whatever. I'm going to get a napkin or something." Noah stalked off.

"I'll go with you," Kacie said, jogging to catch up with him. She touched his elbow and then they disappeared into the mass of campers.

That was not part of my plan. I sighed. I needed to come up with a way to discourage Kacie from Noah without breaking our pact. And fast. She was worse than a leech.

"That was pretty good, Abby."

The voice made me jump. I had forgotten all about Tyler still sitting on the bench Noah had just vacated.

"What?"

He patted the seat next to him. "Perfect payback for the stinkbugs." Tyler had a piece of hair sticking up in back, making him look ornery instead of messy.

I sat on the edge of the bench. "Well, I couldn't just let that slide."

Even sitting, Tyler was a lot taller than me. He was kind of cute though. Not cuter than Noah, but cute.

Tyler laughed. "You're not like most girls, are you?" I didn't reply, instead thinking of a time when Noah had said the very same thing.

"So, any other tricks up your sleeve?" Tyler asked, curiosity making his almond-colored eyes darken.

"Nope."

"Well, I'll be waiting to see," Tyler said as Noah and Kacie returned.

"See what?" Kacie asked, standing close to Noah.

"We were talking about fishing tomorrow," Tyler said. He winked at me. "Noah has claimed to be an avid fisherman."

Was Noah blushing? It was hard to tell in the dim evening light.

"I didn't say that," Noah said. "I just said I've fished before." He shifted slightly away from Kacie.

Kacie smiled up at him. "I've never been fishing. Will you teach me?"

"Sure."

Kacie beamed. I tried not to puke.

"It's really dark out there," Kacie said. "I told Noah about Eddy, and he said he and Tyler would walk with us back to our cabin so we don't get snatched like Eddy." She shivered.

I didn't want to admit how glad I was they were walking us back. Dylan's story had creeped me out.

During the walk, I discovered Tyler was actually pretty fun to talk with, when I wasn't distracted by the giggling coming from Kacie and Noah in front of us. Unfortunately, I only had eyes for Noah. Too bad he was only looking at Kacie.

GO FISH

Kacie and I walked to the rec hall after breakfast, with the rest of our group, for fishing. Noah and Tyler were tossing a football back and forth with the other boys. Noah threw the football to Tyler and then saw us coming. "Kacie!" He waved and jogged over.

"Hey, Noah. Good to see you too," I mumbled under my breath.

Noah glanced at me, and I saw a peculiar glint in his eyes. "Kacie, I just wanted to tell you how much fun I had hanging out with you last night."

My heart deflated like my bicycle tire had when I ran over a nail. "I think I need to ask Esther about the bait we're using today." I turned and headed for Esther and Chad who were surrounded by red pails.

"I'll go with you." Tyler tossed the football toward one of the other boys. When we were out of earshot, he said, "Those two are grossing me out."

"You and me both." I shared a small smile with him.

"Hey, Abby. Good morning, Tyler," Esther said.

"Hey! So what are we using for bait today?" I asked. I was proud of how knowledgeable I sounded.

Chad smiled and held up a pail. "Worms. We're going old school."

"Bet you're too scared to touch those slimy worms," Tyler said. He picked one out of the pail and dangled it in front of me.

I grinned. "My dad and I used to fish all the time when I was younger, so I'm well trained. I won't need any help."

"We'll see about that." Tyler puffed out his chest like he was the man and dropped the worm back in the pail.

I tried not to giggle.

"We're using worms?" Kacie asked, joining us.

"Yup," Esther said, continuing to scoop out worms from a large white bucket and dumping them in the smaller pails.

"Yuck." Kacie wrinkled her nose and glanced at Noah.

He sighed dramatically but looked amused. "I can do that for you too."

Kacie smiled. "I don't like to take the fish off the hook, but Noah already promised to help me."

Wasn't that nice? "Well, I don't mind doing that either, so I can help you too, Kacie," I said. I would do just about anything to keep those two apart.

"Help me carry the pails to the group?" Esther asked, grabbing several red pails herself.

We each grabbed two pails and joined our group.

Chad bounded to the front of the group in a ratty tee shirt and cutoff jean shorts. It seemed like he had unending energy. "All right, guys. It's about a half-mile hike to the fishing pond, so grab a box or bucket of gear, and let's get going."

I held onto the pails I had carried for Esther and followed Chad. Kacie was right behind me. "What kinds of fish are in the pond?" I asked.

"Oh, mostly pickerel. You might find some trout, but the water around here is more suited for pickerel." Chad seemed to know everything about this place.

I nodded like I knew what he was talking about. I had no idea what a pickerel looked like. My dad and I had mostly caught blue gill. Ugly little things. Hopefully, pickerel was a cuter fish.

I chatted with Chad and Kacie as we walked along the forest path. It opened into a clearing filled by a huge pond with weeds growing up around it. Canoes were stacked on a small beach. Fog hung above the water. After hearing Eddy's story, the pond seemed dark and eerie.

"Okay, we'll stop here," Chad said. He set his armful of stuff down. "We'll be here all morning, so just relax and have fun. There should be a pail of worms for each of you, so grab one of those and a pole and pick a spot."

"If you need any help, just ask Chad or me," Esther called out, setting her pails down.

"Or Noah," I muttered.

"What?" Kacie asked.

"Oh, nothing." I coughed a little, hoping she'd think that's what she heard. "I'm going to go find the perfect pole."

Kacie glanced around the group. Everyone was picking out poles and worms. "I'm going to have Noah help me pick. He knows a lot about fishing." She wandered off, swinging her pail of worms.

I took my time choosing a pole, wanting the perfect one. I carried my gear to the spot where Noah, Kacie, and Tyler were setting up. I'd been fishing hundreds of times, but every time I threw my line into the water, I grimaced, thinking someone's eye would get hooked. I shuddered, cast my line, and then sighed in relief when no one started screaming while holding their hand over their eye.

We fished for an hour without catching anything, and I decided to move to a different spot.

"Where are you going?" Kacie asked as I picked up my pail.

"Moving to a different spot so maybe I'll catch something." I stood searching for a spot that wasn't too far away but wasn't close to the others either.

"The fish keep stealing my bait," Tyler said.

I laughed. "Sneaky fish."

Kacie giggled. "They know how to get a meal without being the meal!"

I chose a spot several yards away, but I could still hear Kacie giggling every other second. Clearly, Noah and Kacie were getting along famously. I wished I had packed ear plugs. Trying to block them out, I baited my own hook and threw my line in the water. My mind drifted away, just like my bobber, but it didn't drift to a peaceful place. It drifted to the worst day of my life.

That awful, tragic day kept repeating like some horrible computer clip over and over again in my brain.

"Hey, Abby! I just have to tell you the best news!" Molly was bubbling over with excitement.

"Umm... Okay." I was wondering why my archnemesis wanted to tell me about her exciting news. She should be telling her clones.

Molly had a huge grin on her face, and her eyes sparkled. Her whole presence radiated joy. "Noah just asked me to go to the Winter Dance with him! Isn't that the best news you've ever heard?"

I'd never fainted before, but I thought I was going to after that announcement. No wonder she wanted to share her exciting news with me. I hadn't known what to say. Not that Molly needed a response from me.

"I really thought he was going to ask you since you two are such good friends," she said maliciously. "But Noah said he thought it would be fun if we went together."

When I didn't say anything, she had flounced off to share her *good* news with her friends. I had thought I knew what pain was, but I hadn't until then. I don't know how long I stood in the hallway before I managed to get to my next class. Numbness is all I remember.

After school, Noah was waiting for me in our usual meeting place, but I walked right past him.

"Abby! Wait up!" He raced after me. "What's wrong?"

"What's wrong? You really have to ask me that?" I yelled at him. I crossed my arms and squeezed my backpack straps.

"So you heard about Molly." He stood in front of me, blocking my escape.

"Did you think I wouldn't? It was the biggest news in school today, how you asked Molly." I paused to take a breath. "You couldn't even bother to tell me yourself! But don't worry. I heard from Molly. She made sure of that."

Noah sucked in his breath. "Well, just because you can't go doesn't mean I have to stay home."

"Because clearly you couldn't have come over to my house and hung out with me." In my head, this was exactly what was supposed to happen.

He put his hand on my arm. "Abby, listen."

I flung his hand off me. "No, you listen. I thought we were more than friends. I guess I was wrong. My mistake. Have fun with Molly at the dance. Good-bye, Noah."

After my dramatic speech, I had run off before Noah could see any tears. He had called after me but didn't try to catch up, for which I was grateful. I hadn't wanted him to see me break down. I had cried all night. My parents thought we'd just had a little spat, and it would all blow over. It hadn't.

I wasn't sure why in a million years he had thought asking Molly to the dance would be okay. Noah knew Molly and I didn't get along. She took every opportunity she could to insult me. After the dance, Molly had reminded me everyday how my boyfriend had taken her to the dance instead of me. It was the worst thing Noah could have done to hurt me. The fact that I still liked him made me even angrier. I wanted to hate him, but I couldn't. And that's why it hurt so much. He didn't like me, and he'd used my worst enemy to tell me.

A splash and a shout snapped me out of my daydreaming.

"Abby! Noah's caught a fish!" Kacie shrieked, clapping her hands. "Come look!"

I had to look or I would seem like a jerk, so I laid my pole down and went over. As I got closer, I could see a tiny, spotted, green fish flopping around in the grass. "Cool."

"Isn't it cute?" Kacie practically hugged Noah. "Good job!"

Noah blushed. "Thanks." He laid his pole in the grass and went to rescue his fish. By the time he was gently pulling the hook out, Chad was there to admire his catch.

"It's not very big, but you're the only one to catch anything so far!" Chad said. "Our rule here is 'catch and release,' so go ahead and throw it back in when you're ready."

I think fishes are cool. The zoo aquarium is my favorite place, so I kind of wanted a closer look, but Kacie was worried the fish would die if Noah didn't throw it back in immediately. Not like he would have wanted me to get close enough to see it anyway.

Chad left to go check out some other groups after telling us we had about a half hour before we needed to pack up and head back for camp. As I went back to my spot, Kacie was still gushing over Noah's catch. It was a baby fish, not the Loch Ness Monster. Geez.

After fifteen minutes of blissful silence, I felt a bite. I pulled back on my line and out came a wriggling fish. A thrill of excitement zipped through me. It was kind of disappointing, looking around and realizing no one even knew I'd caught it. I laid my pole down and gripped the squirming, green fish tightly but not forcefully, so I could pull the hook out. I watched its gills go in and out and its tail flap gently. The poor thing was probably scared out of its mind. I walked to the edge of the pond and threw it back in. Then I wiped the fish slime off on my jean shorts. I decided that was enough fishing for me and headed back to Chad and Esther so I'd be ready to go.

As I passed by Noah, he stopped me. "Great catch."

Surprised, I looked up at him. "Thanks." I kept walking, but his quiet praise had shocked me. Noah had been watching me. I had no idea what I should do with that.

DETECTIVE AGENCY

"So what are we going to do during free time?" I asked Kacie as we finished up lunch the next day. The boys were long gone. I swear they inhaled their food.

"I want to talk to Dylan about Eddy," Kacie said. She pressed her paper napkin to her lips like I imagined a queen would at some fancy dinner.

I grinned. "Me too. Think we'll be able to find him?"

Kacie covered her uneaten food with her napkin and stood. "Yup. He could only be at the rec hall, the pool, or the green, so it shouldn't be too hard to find him."

She was right. Our free time was limited to those three places so that should make it easier.

We cleaned up our plates and went to find Dylan. It was pretty easy. He was relaxing in a lounge chair in the open green in the middle of camp.

"What's up, ladies?" Dylan slid his sunglasses on to the top of his head.

"Kacie and I want to know more about Eddy," I said. "Was it just a story you made up or is it really true?"

Dylan folded his hands behind his head. "It's not just a story. It really happened."

Kacie hopped up and down. "A real live mystery!"

"How do you know about Eddy?" I asked.

"Because Eddy is my cousin," Dylan said, sliding his sunglasses back down over his eyes. "Eddy disappeared on camp grounds, and no one knows where he went. That's why I came to camp. I wanted to figure out what happened to him."

"Were there any other clues the police found that you didn't tell us about?" Kacie asked. "I'm determined to help you solve the mystery."

I wanted to help too, but it was hard to take her seriously. I mean, no serious detective would wear a pink ribbon with white trim in her hair.

Dylan thought for a minute. "Well…"

"Well, what?" Kacie asked, tapping the pink toe of her tennis shoe.

"They found a guitar pick in the woods, not far from the pond," Dylan said.

"Really?" I asked.

Kacie's eyes widened. "It was creepy down there."

"We need a notebook and a pencil to keep track of the clues," I said.

"No we don't." Dylan tapped his forehead. "All the clues are right in here."

"So, can we help?" Kacie asked.

"I guess so," Dylan said.

"We're going to need more detectives," Kacie said. "There's Noah and Tyler. Let's ask them if they want to help." She yelled at them to come over.

Noah and Tyler stopped tossing the football they'd been throwing back and forth on the green, and they headed in our direction.

"What's going on?" Noah asked.

I wasn't happy to see them. I didn't want them to help us solve the mystery.

"Remember how we were telling you about Eddy? Dylan said we could help him find Eddy. You guys should help too!" Kacie said.

Noah glanced at Dylan who gave him a nod. "Sounds like fun," Noah said. He smiled at Kacie. "Tossing a football all the time is getting boring."

My shoulders slumped.

Kacie grinned at him. "Absolutely. Dylan just told us the police found a guitar pick in the woods not far from the pond."

"We should go there and see what we can find." Tyler was grinning too.

"Small problem," I said. "We're not allowed in the woods without a counselor present, and if there was anything out there to find, a search team would already have found it."

Tyler nodded. "True. But it would still be kind of cool to look. Maybe they missed something."

"Maybe Chad or Esther would go with us," Kacie said. She moved closer to Noah as if her proximity to him would make us all agree with her.

I shrugged. "It wouldn't hurt to ask."

We found Chad supervising the rec hall. Kacie didn't waste any time asking him if he would go with us.

Chad seemed troubled. "Who told you this story?"

Kacie pointed at Dylan. "Eddy is his cousin."

Chad stared at Dylan, and Dylan shrank under his gaze. Finally, Chad said, "No, I won't go with you in the woods. There's no reason to be out there."

Kacie tried hard to change Chad's mind, but he was firm. Glumly, we left the rec hall.

"Now what?" I asked. I sat down in the grass.

"If Chad said no, Esther will too," Tyler said. He picked a piece of grass and chewed on it. "Maybe one of the other counselors would go with us."

"I doubt it," Dylan said. "Unless we come up with a different reason to go."

Kacie brightened. "We could say we wanted to make a bug collection!"

I rolled my eyes. "Like they would believe that. You wouldn't even touch worms."

She frowned. "Oh. Right."

"We could just go without their permission," Dylan said. He kept his eyes on the ground.

"But we could get kicked out for that!" Kacie said. "We can't!"

I didn't think we should do it either, but I didn't want to leave the mystery unsolved. "Maybe if we just went once."

Noah nodded slowly. "Just once. To see if we can find any clues."

"If we don't, then we won't go again, and no one will ever know," Tyler said.

"I don't know guys," Kacie said. "Maybe we should just forget it." She hugged herself.

"Let's do it!" Dylan grinned. "Let's go find my cousin!"

We walked slowly down the path to the pond. No one even seemed to notice our absence.

Dylan led us into the woods. We stood in a circle, not knowing what to do next.

Kacie broke the silence. "We should stick together." She linked arms with Noah.

They looked cute together—her pink shirt and his gray one side by side. Gag me.

"Let's go this way," Dylan said.

Noah and Kacie followed.

"I guess that leaves us," I said to Tyler.

"After you." He motioned me with his hand.

"What if whoever took Eddy takes us?" I whispered, letting the others move a little ahead. I didn't want Noah to know I was scared.

"One person against five?" Tyler asked. He held a tree branch back for me.

"Maybe he wasn't taken by one person. Maybe he was taken by a gang of masked bandits. They wait for kids to sneak into the woods and then they pounce. Maybe that's why we're not allowed in here." I was seriously afraid now.

"A gang of masked bandits? You're weird." He checked underneath a bush for clues.

I ignored his comment and kept looking around for bandits.

"Look what I found!" Tyler exclaimed.

I jumped and then felt embarrassed when I saw him holding up a muddy tennis shoe by its dirty, wet shoelace.

"That doesn't look like it was lost five years ago. More like a couple of weeks," I said, wrinkling my nose. I didn't even want to know what it smelled like.

He threw it back into the forest. "How does somebody lose a shoe in the woods, anyway?"

"Stepping in quicksand?" I smiled to myself.

"Or maybe a professional tree climber was trying to climb the highest tree in the woods, but when he got halfway, a panther attacked him and took his shoe." Tyler growled and made cat claws with his fingers.

I giggled. "A panther? In the woods?"

He shrugged. "It's more believable than your quicksand. Or your gang of masked bandits."

He had a point.

After ten minutes of unsuccessful searching, Tyler and I caught up with the others. We decided to call it quits and hike back to camp.

"You might want to clean up your face," Tyler told Noah.

Noah had a big streak of dirt across his forehead. He swiped at his face with his shirt sleeve.

"Sorry I made you move that log for a plastic chip bag," Kacie said. Her eyes showed her disappointment.

"Stop! Stop, guys!" Dylan shouted.

I covered my ears with my hands. Dylan's deep voice was loud!

Dylan proudly held up a faded blue guitar pick. "Eddy was here!"

"Can I see it?" I held out my hand, and Dylan gave me his find.

I studied the guitar pick and knew right away it was old. It was dirty, covered in layers of grime from having been on the ground and out in the weather. "Wow. This could really be Eddy's."

Dylan snatched it back. "I think it is." He gave the pick to Noah. "What do you think?"

Noah looked up at me and then at Kacie. "I think so too."

Kacie wore a triumphant smile. "We actually found something!"

"Now what?" I asked.

"We have to search again," Dylan said. "Clearly, Eddy was here."

Tyler and Noah looked at each other.

"I don't want to get in trouble, but I want to search again," Kacie said. "Maybe we should give the pick to a counselor."

I snorted. "And tell them what? That we found it in the woods when we snuck in by ourselves?"

"We have to make a pact," Dylan said.

Great another pact. At least this one was legit.

Dylan put his hand in the center of our circle. "No one says a word about this."

I put my hand on top of his and then Tyler and Noah put their hands in. Kacie finally put hers in too.

When she did, we heard a horn blowing.

Kacie gasped. "Free time is over!"

We ran out of the woods and back up the hill. Kacie grabbed my hand and dragged me to the line of girls waiting to be led back to our cabins.

"We made it!" Kacie said.

I was struggling to breathe normally.

Kacie waved at the boys who had made it to their line too. "That was close." She glanced down at her grubby clothes and then at mine. "We're going to need to change before supper."

I couldn't figure out how Kacie could switch so quickly from escaping trouble to her wardrobe. Claire and I would be giggling over our close call.

"I want to fix my hair. Make it look cute for Noah." Kacie let go of my hand and followed the girls in front of her.

I felt a familiar tug at my heart. Once upon a time, I had wanted to look pretty for Noah too. Now he wouldn't even notice if I tried. "Your hair is pretty the way it is," I said. "You don't need to fix it for jerk Noah."

Kacie stopped in her tracks. "Jerk Noah?"

"Umm..." I fumbled for an answer. "Well, he doesn't seem very nice, putting stinkbugs in my hair."

Kacie wrinkled her nose. "I forgot about that." She waved her hand in dismissal. "It was just a joke."

"To him, maybe. To me, it was a jerk thing to do." I shuddered, thinking about those creepy crawlies in my hair. Yuck!

Kacie stopped suddenly and put a hand on her hip. "I think you're jealous."

I could feel the color drain from my face. "Jealous? What are you talking about? I'm not jealous."

Kacie waved her finger at me. "Oh, yes you are. You wish Tyler would notice you the way Noah has noticed me. That's why you think Noah's a jerk."

Relief washed over me. She thought I was jealous because I didn't have a boyfriend. I guess that was kind of true, just not in the way she thought.

"Well, you're just going to have to get over it," she said with a stern, teacher look on her face.

I pushed past her. "Okay. I'll try."

Kacie came up beside me and put her arm around me. "Don't worry. If Tyler doesn't work out, some other boy here will."

The rest of the way to the cabin, which was thankfully not long, Kacie chatted about the different boys she'd met and then rejected every one as a possibility for me. Apparently, there was no one here that was right for me. Not that I didn't already know that. If I wasn't so completely furious with him, Noah would be the only boy I wanted. No one else even came close.

I opened the screen door and headed straight for our bunk, dodging other girls who were trying to change before supper too. When I got to our bunks, the rankest smell ever hit my nose.

"What is that?" Kacie asked, pinching her nose with her fingers.

"I have no idea." After checking under our sleeping bags, I got on my hands and knees and peeked under the bed. In between our suitcases was a small pile of pond scum. No wonder it smelled fishy.

"I think I'm going to puke," Kacie said, kneeling next to me. Her face was pea green.

"One of us has to pick this up and take it outside," I said. Somehow, I knew it was going to be me.

Kacie looked appalled. "I'm not touching that."

I sighed. "Fine. I'll do it."

She swallowed hard and sat down.

I slid my suitcase out from under the bed, opened it, and grabbed a used pair of socks. After pulling them onto my hands, I scooped up the pile of pond muck. Kacie ran in front of me to open the screen door, and I tossed the muck over the railing. I took my socks off my hands and threw them over the railing too. No way was I putting those smelly things in my suitcase.

"Who would have done this?" Kacie asked me when I came back in the cabin. She sat down on her bed. "It's just plain mean."

"Oh, I know who," I said, sitting next to her. "Noah. And probably Tyler."

"They wouldn't do that. Especially Noah." Kacie was still pinching her nose. "Besides, we aren't allowed in the cabins during free time."

I looked around and saw that Esther was chatting with one of the other girls. "We aren't allowed in the woods either."

She paled.

"How are we going to get them back?" Ideas were racing around in my brain. "Underwear on the flag pole?"

Kacie stood up. "Noah wouldn't do that. He played one joke on you and apologized. He wouldn't do this."

I shook my head in frustration. Fine. Kacie could believe all she wanted that Noah was innocent, but I knew he was the culprit, and I was going to get him back. I'd come up with something, and I would do it without Kacie's help.

HEAVY HEARTS

Thursday, I finally had the opportunity to talk to Noah alone, and I took it. Kacie had gotten permission to run back to the cabin to get her favorite pink sweatshirt before campfire and Noah was relaxing in a chair in the green. Tyler was tossing a ball with Chad and some other boys, so I sat on the edge of the chair next to Noah and pointed my finger at him.

"Kacie thinks you can do no wrong, but I know better. I know it was you and probably Tyler who hid that stinky pond muck in our cabin." I paused to take a breath.

"Abby..."

"No, you don't get to talk"—I waved my finger at him—"I will get you and Tyler back. You can count on it."

Noah's eyes sparkled. "It was a great prank, huh?"

It was a great prank, but I wasn't about to tell him that. "I'll get you back worse."

Noah laughed. "You can't top that! No way."

I put my hands on my hips. "Wanna bet?"

"I'll bet you a twist ice cream cone with blue eyes that you can't top that prank," Noah said.

My heart pounded like a thousand bongo drums. Twist ice cream was my favorite and he knew it.

Noah held out his hand. "Deal?"

I stared at his hand and tried to remind myself I was still mad at him.

"What's going on?" Kacie asked, glancing back and forth between us.

In the heat of the moment, neither Noah nor I had seen her returning.

Noah dropped his hand. "Abby and I were talking about Eddy. I was reminding her of our pact."

I coughed and tried to roll with the story Noah had come up with on the fly. "Yeah. I'm feeling bad about what we did."

Kacie nodded. "Me too. But we did make a pact, Abby. We have to stick together. We just won't do it again."

Noah smiled at Kacie. "That's exactly right." All his attention was directed at her now.

"I'm going to talk to Tyler," I said. I walked over to Tyler who was playing catch with one of his cabinmates. "Hey."

"What's up? The two lovebirds grossing you out?" he asked without taking his eyes off the football.

I nodded. "How'd you guess?"

"Noah said he wanted to hang out with Kacie after supper." Tyler caught the ball and threw it to Brian. "I think he's going to ask her to the dance."

"Oh," I said.

Tyler glanced at me quickly and then back to the ball. He caught it again and threw it back. "You sound sad about that."

"What? Sad? No. Why would I be sad?" I asked, hoping to cover my reaction. I'd already known he wouldn't ask me to the dance. A girl could hope though. Not that I would have said yes. I mean after what he did to me, I would definitely have said no.

Tyler stretched to catch the ball. "I was hoping you weren't in love with Noah, because it sure seems like all the other girls are."

I snorted loudly to cover up my confusion. "No. Why would I be?" He was just cute, funny, had a dimple... There was nothing to like about him at all.

"Good. So wanna hang out at the campfire?" Tyler asked, giving me a quick smile before throwing the ball.

"Sure." Hanging out with Tyler would be much more fun than watching Kacie drool all over Noah.

Brian caught the football off a bounce. "Great. Now that we have that all worked out, maybe we could play catch."

I backed away with my hands up, palms out. "Sorry. I didn't realize this was such a serious game."

"Do you want to play, Abs?" Tyler asked.

I smiled but shook my head no. Normally, I wasn't into nicknames, since technically Abby was already a nickname, but Tyler made it sound cute, and it was nice to have him want to hang out with me. I wandered over to Esther. No need to find Kacie and hear about how Noah had asked her to the dance. Esther was sitting on a stone bench, head in her hands.

I tapped her on the shoulder.

She flinched, looked up, and then smiled. "Abby. You scared me. What's up?"

"Are you okay?" I sat down on the bench next to her.

"I'm fine. I'm giving devotion tonight, so I was just praying," she said. She ran her hands through her hair. "I like to pray before."

I'd seen Pastor Rick pray before we had a rally or youth meeting. "Sure. So what is tonight about?"

"Forgiveness," Esther said. She closed the Bible lying on her lap. "I keep coming to it in my Bible, so that's what it's going to be on." She looked around. "Not hanging out with your friends?"

I shrugged. "No."

"Oh. I see." She rubbed her hands on her jeans and then stood up, laying her Bible on the bench. "Want to help me get the fire going?"

"Sure."

Esther signaled to Chad, and he nodded.

When we arrived at the campfire site, Esther walked over to the pit and peered in. "We're going to need a bit of everything. Why don't you look for some smaller twigs and sticks while I get some of the bigger stuff from the pile? Just don't go too far into the woods, okay?"

I tried not to cringe at the reminder to not wander off. We weren't going to go again, so no harm done. "No problem." I moved just inside the line of trees and began picking up small sticks. When I couldn't cradle any more in my arms, I went back to the fire pit.

Esther had the big logs set up like a teepee. She looked up when she heard my footsteps. "Perfect timing." She motioned me to set my load down next to the pit. "A few of your twigs" — she picked up a handful and tossed them into the center of the teepee — "And now to light it." She pulled a yellow lighter out of her jeans pocket.

"You're not going to rub sticks together to get it started?" I asked.

She laughed. "Not tonight."

The fire started up after Esther blew gently on the small flame. "That should do it." She stood up and brushed off her hands. "Just in time too."

I turned around and saw campers straggling in. "I should find our group."

"Right there." Esther pointed. "Thanks for your help." She turned to watch the flickering flames.

I left to join my group. Tyler stood up and waved his hands. Not that he needed to. Just standing made him stick out in the crowd since he was so tall. I ran up the stairs and sat down. "Thanks for saving me a seat."

He pulled a plastic baggie out of his shorts pocket and dangled it in front of me. "Candy?"

My eyes widened when I saw the colorful candy. "That's contraband!"

His eyes twinkled. "Don't tell." He lowered the bag. "Want some?"

"Uh, yeah!" I grabbed a couple of pieces of the candy and stuck them into my mouth. "Mmmm…" Chewy, fruity sweetness hit my taste buds.

"Aren't you glad I brought it?" Tyler asked, sitting down. He stuck some of the candy in his mouth.

I swallowed. "Yup."

"More?" He held the bag out to me again.

I shook my head. "Thanks, though."

He took another handful and then put the bag back into his pocket.

"Aren't those going to melt?" I asked.

Tyler shrugged. "Whatever. They're in a bag. I have more."

Esther stood up, stuck two fingers in her mouth, and whistled shrilly. Everyone settled down. "Tonight we're going to talk about a topic that's pretty serious. I want to talk to you about forgiveness. Raise your hand if you have ever been hurt by a friend, a family member, a classmate, or maybe even someone here at camp?" She raised her hand.

I raised my hand just a little, not wanting to be the only one who did.

"Now look around you," she said.

Looking around, I saw that almost every camper had their hand raised.

Esther smiled and lowered her hand. "Okay, you can put your hands down. Everyone here has been hurt by someone, and that's why forgiveness is so important. If we don't forgive the people who have hurt us, we start becoming bitter and angry. No one likes to be around a person who's angry all the time."

That was true. I had an aunt who was awfully mean. Even her face looked like she was sucking on a sour gummy worm.

"Tonight, I want to focus on a verse that we've probably all said, heard, or read a hundred times but never really thought about. It's in Matthew chapter 6, verse 12 from the Lord's Prayer." Esther paused to flip open a small, pink Bible and then read. "And forgive us our debts, as we forgive our debtors."

I recognized the verse right away.

"Can anyone tell me what this verse means?" Esther looked around for volunteers.

This time no one raised their hands.

"It means we will be forgiven to the degree we forgive. Do you remember the people who hurt you?" she asked.

Noah. No problem remembering that.

"If you haven't forgiven them, then you haven't been forgiven for your sins either," Esther said. She paused to let that statement sink in.

And sink in it did. I glanced at Tyler, who appeared absorbed in what Esther was saying. That couldn't be true, could it? I blinked. No way.

"Don't believe me?" Esther asked. I swear she looked right at me. "Then listen to verses 14 and 15, 'For if ye forgive men their trespasses, your heavenly Father will also forgive you: But if ye forgive not men their trespasses, neither will your Father forgive your trespasses.'"

I didn't remember reading that in the Bible, ever. She had to be making this all up.

"You see why it's so important to forgive? If you want to be forgiven, you have to forgive. I know it's hard. The person who hurt you may not deserve to be forgiven. They might not have apologized to you, or even know they hurt you, but there's something else we need to think about. Raise your hand if you've ever hurt anyone." Esther raised her hand again.

I raised mine too. I didn't even want to think about all the people I'd hurt. Mom, Dad, Kent, Claire, Mrs. Wrinklesteen…

"Look around and see all the hands raised." Esther paused so we could look. "Every one of us has hurt someone. There's a good chance we don't deserve to be forgiven. The Bible is clear. We need to forgive."

I felt like one of those stone statues in fancy gardens, pretty to look at but cold all the way through. There was no way I was going to forgive Noah. No stinkin' way. What he did was unforgiveable. Surely, God knew some things were beyond forgiveness.

"I'm going to pray now and then Denton is going to play some songs on his guitar. Feel free to sing along if you know the words." Esther bowed her head, as did Tyler beside me. I sat stick straight.

"Father, I know we all have some big hurts in our lives, and sometimes, it feels like it's impossible to forgive the people who caused them, but your word is clear. You want us to forgive. Give us the strength to make the choice to forgive and to keep forgiving that person over and over again. Thank you for forgiving us. In Jesus's name we pray. Amen." Esther quickly sat down and let Denton take over.

Denton strummed his guitar and a soft melody drifted toward me. I recognized the song from church but didn't sing along.

Okay, fine. Maybe what Esther said was true. Maybe I did need to forgive Noah. He had apologized. More than once. Well, he'd tried to apologize, but I hadn't really let him. Besides, Esther said that unforgiveness led to anger and bitterness.

Wait, though. Sure I was angry sometimes, but not all the time. I didn't look like I was sucking on a sour gummy worm, so I didn't need to worry. The quiet music enveloped me as I thought about my situation. Even if I did forgive Noah, it wasn't going to change anything. He wouldn't miraculously like me again. Forgiving him wouldn't automatically heal my hurt. So what was the point? If I didn't see any signs of bitterness in my life, which I didn't, then I didn't need to forgive him. I could hear sniffles around me, but my heart was an ice cube in my chest. I didn't feel even a drop of forgiveness. Not one.

Tyler elbowed me, and I jumped. "Don't know any of the songs?" he whispered.

"I do," I replied quickly. "I was just thinking."

Tyler looked at me curiously. "Oh." He patted his shorts pocket. "Need any thinking candy?"

I tried to smile. "No, I'm done thinking now." I turned toward the fire and joined in singing with the other campers, but my heart wasn't in it. Even when one of my favorite songs began, I felt nothing. I would never forgive Noah. Not as long as I lived.

MUDDY WATERS

"I'm so excited about creek stomping today!" Kacie said, tightening her curly ponytail.

I looked at her pristine white tennis shoes. "Are you sure you want to wear those?"

Kacie glanced down. "Oh, these are my old tennis shoes. I've had them forever."

My old shoes were a grayish-brown color with scuffs, and the shoelaces were falling apart. The sole had a flap you could lift up and see through to my socks. They probably should have been thrown away a long time ago, but now I was glad I'd saved them. I could just pitch them after creek stomping.

Kacie lowered her voice. "Noah said we might find another clue about Eddy." She took her ponytail holder out and started over. Kacie was worse than Claire when it came to her hair.

I rolled my eyes before sitting down on the bunk bed. If I heard another "Noah said" comment, I thought I was going to vomit. "I hope you do."

Kacie smiled and looked at me through her handheld mirror. "I know Dylan isn't going to be with us, but I think we should look anyway."

"It's a good time to look." I stood up, banging the top of my head on the bunk above me. "Ouch!" I rubbed my head.

"I just hope Dylan doesn't feel left out," Kacie said, without even acknowledging my bruised head. She'd seen me conk my head on that bed many times already.

"I don't think he will. Are you ready yet?" I started for the door. The other girls were lining up behind Esther. "We're just going to get muddy and gross anyway."

Kacie smiled one more time into the mirror and put it down. "Yup. Think Noah will like this outfit?" She twirled around in a royal blue romper. Way too new to go creek stomping in, but whatever. At least it wasn't pink.

I sighed. "I'm sure he'll love it. Let's go." I waved her toward the door. "The sooner we leave, the sooner you'll see Noah, not that I know why you really want to."

Kacie followed me down the cabin steps. "Well, he's nice, and sweet, and he has a dimple when he smiles."

I just about choked. That was my dimple, thank you very much. I felt like one of those rusty fish hooks was trying to yank out my heart. "Yes, well, he did put pond muck in our cabin. Let's not forget that."

"He did not."

"He did too, Kace. Noah's just like all of the other boys here." He really was the same. I'd learned that the hard way.

Kacie giggled. "Well you know what they say about boys who pick on girls."

I groaned. "Just so you know, whoever made that up was seriously deranged. It's not true."

Kacie's face lit with compassion. "You got dumped."

I looked at her in shock. "What? Who said anything about getting dumped?"

"I get it now." She put her hand on my arm. "All the bitterness and 'boys are jerks' stuff. You got dumped. I don't know how I missed it." Kacie stopped and stared into my eyes. "Tell me about it."

Now I was embarrassed and a little bit angry. I didn't need Kacie's pity. "It's nothing, really."

"Clearly, it is or you wouldn't be this bitter." Kacie didn't budge from her spot on the path, causing other campers to veer around us.

"I really liked this guy, and I thought he liked me too. It didn't work out. Whatever." I pulled my arm from her grasp and kept walking toward the spot where we were supposed to meet. That's all psychiatrist Kacie was getting.

"What happened?" she asked, following me.

"I was just wrong about him liking me. End of story."

Kacie made a horrified noise that sounded kind of like a scared dog. When I glanced at her, she had tears in her eyes. She linked her arm with mine. "You're better off without him. I'm so glad Noah's not like that."

For the second time, I almost choked.

In a flash, Kacie's tears were replaced with twinkles. "I didn't want to say anything, but you and Tyler looked pretty friendly last night. Noah and I both noticed."

My eyes widened. "Tyler? Me?" I shook my head. "No. We're just friends."

"That's not what it looked like to Noah and me," she said. "Well, more me than Noah. Now that I think about it, Noah didn't really say much."

My heart zinged. Could Noah be jealous?

Kacie shrugged. "He was pretty quiet all day, except for when we talked about the dance."

And now my heart brought me back to reality. It was silly for me to have thought Noah might be jealous. "I promise Tyler and I are just friends, and that's all."

Kacie smiled, those white teeth flashing. "We'll see about that."

I had never been so relieved to see the boys. They were standing by the creek bank in scrubby clothes. Chad's shirt had so many holes in it; he might as well not have been wearing one. He needed to take lessons from Esther. She managed to look nice even though you could tell her tee shirt and shorts were old. Maybe someday, I could have her sense of style. Even Claire would be impressed.

"Glad you girls could make it," Chad said, grinning from ear to ear. "Now that we're all here, I hope you're wearing your oldest clothes because we are going to get dirty!"

The boys cheered.

I glanced again at Kacie's white shoes and blue romper.

"So let's get in!" Chad jumped in, causing droplets of dirty creek water to splash over us.

"Eww!" several of the girls shrieked.

The boys jumped in with a whoop. Kacie and I weren't far behind. Several of the girls were just putting their toes in and Esther was trying to encourage them to hop in. The water was cool, but definitely not icy. Those girls were just being chicken.

"Follow me!" Chad called, stomping his way down the creek.

Kacie was stomping with gusto. She grinned. "Isn't this fun?"

I couldn't disagree. The cool water felt good, even if it was filthy and only came up to my knees.

"Let's catch up with Noah and Tyler," Kacie said.

I didn't want to, but I couldn't tell Kacie no. It would have been like taking a bone from a puppy. So we stomped faster to catch up with them.

"Ladies." Tyler pretended to take a hat off his head and gave us a sweeping bow.

Kacie giggled and turned her attention to Noah.

I blocked them out and gave Tyler a shove. "Show-off."

He jumped up, kicked his heels together, and then splashed down.

I laughed while wiping dirty creek water from my face. "Nice."

"You try it." Tyler jumped again, displaying his trick. "See, it's easy."

I backed away. "No thanks."

"Just try," he said; those almond-colored eyes pleading with me.

I took a deep breath and jumped. I tried to kick my heels together, but I was pretty sure by the sound of Tyler's laughter that they just flapped around.

"What are you guys doing?" Noah asked, wading over to us.

Tyler demonstrated his skill again.

Pretty soon, all four of us were jumping and kicking our heels together, or at least trying to, laughing as we splashed each other.

Noah landed near me, spraying water all over me. I turned my face to keep water from getting in my eyes.

"That was a good one!" Noah gave Tyler a high-five.

I giggled. Then I froze. Wait a minute. Noah and I weren't friends. I wasn't supposed to be having fun with him like nothing had ever happened.

Noah grinned at me. His blondish-brown hair spiked up in the back; his dimple out in full force.

I frowned at him, trying to make my eyes tiny slits and stomped away, following the sound of girls shrieking. The other campers had passed us as we were practicing Tyler's trick.

"Party-pooper," Noah mumbled as he stomped past me, Kacie not far behind.

I stomped even harder. What did he expect? To be best friends again? I don't think so. He'd done way too much for that to happen.

Tyler came up beside me. He was tall enough that the water only came to his shins. "Whoa! What did the creek do to you?"

"None of your business, okay?" I said, continuing to stomp as if my life depended on it.

Instead of backing off, Tyler kept pace with me. "Are you sure you and Noah don't have a thing? Because sometimes you sure act like you do."

I ignored the question and kept stomping. Tyler stomped right next to me, seemingly unconcerned with the fact that I hadn't answered him.

"Abby! Come look at the minnows I found!" Kacie called. Noah stood next to her, looking at the water.

I rolled my eyes. Really? Now I was supposed to be excited about minnows. I waded over. "Cool."

"Aren't they so cute?" She poked her finger in the water trying to touch them and giggled as they darted away.

"Adorable," I said, barely holding in my sarcasm. What was wrong with me? Normally, I would think minnows were pretty cool too.

Kacie stood up and snapped her fingers. "I totally forgot."

"About what?" Noah asked. He stopped watching the minnows and looked at Kacie.

"I haven't been looking for Eddy clues," Kacie said, frowning. "Some detective I am."

"We still have time to find something," Noah said. He smiled at her.

Why did Noah like Kacie so much? Silly question. I knew why. Pretty curly hair, big brown eyes, a blinding white smile, sweet personality...I stopped myself and took a deep breath. Kacie was a sweet girl. She was my friend too, I reminded myself. Most of the time. When

I wasn't trying to puke at her attempts to snag Noah or when—

"What do you say, Abby?" Tyler asked, throwing his arm around me. "Want to put your detective hat back on?"

I wasn't going to turn down a chance to solve the mystery. Maybe then Noah would pay attention to me. "Sure!"

"That's my girl." Tyler grinned that charming grin of his and immediately began searching the slightly murky water.

Noah glared at Tyler before wading to the creek bank. He picked up a rock and then set it back down.

Kacie clapped her hands. "This will be so much fun!"

Oh boy, I thought, but I leaned over the creek water to look too. I hoped I found something good.

I peered down at the water, not really paying attention to where I was going, when *smack*! My legs hit the edge of the creek bed. Graceful, coordinated girls would have been able to catch themselves, but me, well, my hands didn't react quickly enough, and I landed face first in the squishy mud; my behind sticking up in the air. "Oof."

I heard an "oh my gosh" from Kacie and the sounds of splashing as they all came toward me. I sighed as I lifted my head from the mud. My face grew hot as I pushed myself up. Good thing it was covered in mud.

"Are you okay?" Kacie asked, arriving first. Noah and Tyler weren't far behind.

"I'm fine," I said, trying to play it cool. I leaned over and used creek water to wash the mud off my face.

Tyler was laughing uncontrollably. I couldn't tell if he had tears running down his cheeks or if it was just creek water. "I wish I would have had a video camera! That was so funny!"

"You missed a spot." Noah reached out his fingers to wipe mud off my chin. "Oops, it just smeared."

I couldn't move. Couldn't breathe.

"A little water will get that right off," Kacie said, pushing Noah to the side. She rubbed her wet finger on my chin. "All better."

I unlocked my eyes from Noah's, breaking the spell between us. "Thanks, Kacie."

Tyler held up a hand, still laughing. "Dude! Let me reenact it for you."

"Uh, how about not." I used my shirt sleeve to wipe a drip on my forehead.

He ignored me and did the reenactment anyway. I had to admit it was pretty funny.

"Wasn't that great?" Tyler asked. He was still chuckling.

I smacked him on the shoulder. "I'll probably have some very colorful bruises tomorrow, and all you can do is laugh. I could have suffocated!" Maybe I exaggerated a bit, but you never know.

Tyler tried to compose himself but couldn't.

"Let's keep looking for clues, guys," Kacie said. "I can't hear anyone else anymore, so we must be really far behind. We need to catch up."

Kacie and I left the boys behind.

As I shuffled through the water, I paid a little more attention to where I was going, but my mind was still on that moment when Noah wiped the mud off my chin. I couldn't deny that I still liked him. It was just easier to be mad than to deal with his betrayal. Sadness washed over me. Why had he asked Molly to the dance and ruined everything?

A splash of water startled me. Chad appeared around the bend. "What's going on, guys?" He was completely drenched and muddy from head to toe.

"We're looking for—"

"For frogs and crayfish." I shot Kacie a look.

Her eyes widened, and then she nodded vigorously. "Yup. Frogs and crayfish."

"Well, the rest of the group is done," Chad said. "They're getting hosed down and dried off, so we need to get you guys going." He slicked back his shaggy wet hair.

Kacie looked disappointed. "Okay."

Chad bounded off—well, as fast you can bounce in the water, and Kacie and I did our best to keep up. We got out of the creek and allowed Esther to spray us off.

Tyler and Noah climbed out of the creek shortly after us, and Tyler came right to me. "Did you guys find anything?"

I shook my head and grabbed a towel from a pile on the ground. "Go get cleaned up. They're waiting on us." I was just as disappointed as Kacie. Would we ever find out what happened to Eddy?

Tyler let Esther hose him off, after pushing Noah out of the spray. Noah shoved him, and the two jostled each other, laughing until Esther declared they were clean.

I shook my head. Boys.

"Bad news," Kacie said, running over to me.

"What?" I twisted the towel around my hair.

"Chad says we won't be back in the woods for a couple of days," Kacie said, frustration dulling her brown eyes.

"We'll figure something out," I replied, more concerned about my wet feet. It was not going to be a fun walk back to the cabin in my squishy shoes.

"I'm going to tell Noah and Tyler." She ran over to the boys.

Would we have to sneak back in the woods to solve Dylan's mystery? Even though I knew we shouldn't, excitement zipped through me. I still wished I was in Italy with Claire, but this detective work was making camp bearable. One more time in the woods wouldn't hurt anything. Just one more time.

FRENEMY

"I LOVE WORKING WITH clay!" Kacie exclaimed the next afternoon as we waited for the boys to show up for more clue-finding in the woods.

Kacie was referring to our arts and crafts session this morning. She had been able to mold her clay into a cool bowl. As soon as they dried and were baked, we would be able to paint them. My lopsided bowl didn't look anything like hers. I was beginning to think there wasn't anything Kacie couldn't do. It was a good thing she was so sweet, or she would be annoying. Well, she was kind of annoying anyway.

I smiled when I thought of Tyler's project. "Did you see Tyler's turtle?"

Kacie giggled. "Is that what it was?"

"Hey! Don't make fun of my turtle!" Tyler said, coming up behind us.

"It looked a little more like a blob than a turtle," Noah said, grinning.

"Like yours was any better," Tyler said, slapping Noah on the back. "Was yours supposed to be an airplane? Because it looked more like a cross."

Noah slapped him back. The two continued to razz each other, playfully shoving back and forth.

I ducked my head as a stray raindrop plopped on my head and trickled down my forehead. Looking up, I discovered I was standing under a tree limb that was still wet from the earlier downpour. Thankfully, it wasn't raining now. There's nothing more miserable than traipsing around in wet clothes, especially wet jeans. I looked down at my jeans and wished I had thought to bring an umbrella or something. Fortunately, the threat of rain had kept most of the kids in the rec hall, making it easier for us to sneak off.

Dylan finally joined us, wearing some crazy, blue zebra sneakers. "You guys ready to hunt for Eddy?"

"Let's go!" Kacie jumped up and down. "I have a feeling we're going to find something big."

We all shushed her, except for Dylan. He smiled at her. "You never know." He looked at the rest of us. "I think we should go by the creek this time."

We hiked next to the creek and I enjoyed the fresh smell of the woods. It was much better than the wormy smell at home after it rained.

After a few minutes of walking, Dylan stopped us. "I think we should split up," he said. "We can meet back here."

Kacie rubbed her arms. It was kind of chilly. I was grateful for my comfy long, sleeve shirt. My mom and I had argued about packing it. She'd won in the end. I wouldn't tell her I'd actually needed it.

"I think Noah should come with me, and Tyler and Abby should go together," Kacie said. "Dylan, you can come with me and Noah."

Before she went off with them, Kacie whispered, "Maybe today will be the day Noah and Tyler ask us to the dance."

"I thought we were hunting for Eddy clues, not trying to score dates for the dance," I whispered back. I doubted Noah would ask Kacie in front of Dylan. Talk about awkward!

"True, but if we get dates, that would be even better." Her eyes twinkled.

I waved my hand. "Just go. Just go with Noah."

My heart pinched when Kacie grabbed Noah's hand, but he quickly dropped it as they tramped into the woods.

"So what are we looking for, exactly?" Tyler asked, standing next to me.

"I don't know," I said. "Something that belonged to Eddy? Like dirty shoes?"

We shared a smile.

"Well, let's just look for anything out of the ordinary," Tyler said.

The nice thing about Tyler was that I didn't have to pretend with him. I could just be me.

"It's so sad the police couldn't find Eddy." I stepped into the woods. "It's so weird that Eddy disappeared here."

Tyler shrugged. "It's kind of fun."

"Fun?" I asked, raising my eyebrows.

"Well, being detectives is kind of fun." Tyler stepped over a log.

"Speaking of detective work, did you help Noah put the pond muck in our cabin?" I asked. I scuffed the toe of my shoe in the wet dirt.

"Whoa! That's a random question," Tyler said, giving me a quick glance.

"Well, did you?"

He grinned. "What do you think?" He kicked at a dead leaf, but the morning rain had it plastered on the ground.

"Mmm..." I pushed a branch from a sapling out of my way. "You know I'm going to get you guys back, right?" I let it spring back just in front of him, so water droplets sprayed him.

Tyler laughed. "I think you just did." He wiped his face. "So you and Kacie aren't going to team up against us?"

I snorted. "Kacie doesn't think perfect Noah would pull a prank on us. I think in her head she thinks the pond muck oozed there all by itself." I paused. "Just know I'll come up with something way better."

"I'm counting on it." He shook a branch at me.

I smacked him and then dried my face off with my sleeve. "Whatever."

He probably didn't think I could do it, but I knew I would come up with something brilliant, and something that would get Noah back good. Noah was going down.

"Hey! What's that?" Tyler asked, pointing to a green patch, just barely sticking out of a thick bush.

We hiked over to the bush.

"What is it?" I asked as Tyler tugged at the patch.

"I don't know." He grunted with his effort. "This bush has thorns."

I watched Tyler struggle with the bush. "I think the bush is winning."

Tyler stuck his tongue out at me before resuming his tugging. He stopped and wiped his forehead. "I think it might be easier to stick my arm in there and untangle it." Streaks of dirt decorated his yellow tee shirt.

"My arm is skinnier," I said. I wasn't afraid of a little hard work.

Tyler thought about it and then agreed. He sat down on a fallen log. "Have at it."

I studied the bush and looked for the widest opening. After picking a spot, I carefully stuck my arm in, but not carefully enough. "Ouch! These thorns are sharp!"

"Thorns usually are," Tyler said. He didn't sound sorry for me at all.

"Thanks for the encouragement." I refocused on the bush. Several minutes and scratches later, I had a soggy, faded, green ball cap in my hand. "It looks really old." I wrung it out.

"It sure does." Tyler took the hat. "Do you think it's Eddy's?"

"Maybe. Let's find Dylan and see." I wiped my hands on my jeans in nervous anticipation. Had we just found a clue?

"Yup. Let's go." Tyler held the baseball cap as we walked back to our meeting spot.

"Do you see them?" I asked. They couldn't be too far.

Tyler pointed into the woods, and I could just barely see Kacie's pinky-orange shirt. Sometimes, her love for pink came in handy.

"Let's go catch up with them," I said. I didn't wait to see if he would follow me before I took off for Kacie and Noah.

I crashed through the underbrush toward the patch of pink shirt. When I got close enough to see Kacie's bouncy ponytail, I yelled, "Did you guys find anything?"

Kacie held up a hand. "Another guitar pick!" She lowered it and asked, "What about you guys? Find anything?"

"We think so." Tyler held up the hat. "Dylan, does this look like Eddy's?"

Dylan looked shocked. He reached for the hat. "Eddy loved this hat. He wore it all the time." He held it carefully. "Where did you find this?"

"In a bush back there," I said. I couldn't believe we had just found something the police had missed.

"We should definitely show this to a counselor," Kacie said.

Dylan's head whipped around. "We made a pact, remember?"

"I don't know, Dylan," Tyler said. "I think Kace is right."

"But we could get kicked out of camp," Dylan said.

I didn't know what to do. I really wanted to solve the case, but maybe the hat should go to the proper authorities.

"Let's just keep this between us. Please?" Dylan was begging.

"Don't you want Eddy to be found?" Noah asked. "The police know what they're doing."

Kacie nodded.

Dylan smirked. "Obviously not, since they couldn't find him five years ago." He looked down at the hat. "It's just that this was Eddy's favorite hat, and they'll make me give it back to them as evidence."

My mind was made up. "I'll keep it a secret, but if we find anything else, we have to tell a counselor."

Everyone agreed.

"We should get going," Dylan said.

"It's probably getting close to dinner." Noah rubbed his stomach. "I'm hungry."

"Me too!" Tyler exclaimed. "We're having pizza tonight! I don't want to miss that!"

"Lead the way," I said, sweeping my arm across my body.

Tyler took the lead and we followed him back to camp. Kacie kept asking Dylan questions about Eddy and his mysterious disappearance, but Dylan only repeated the same information.

What had happened to Eddy? Was he still lost in the woods searching for home? I hoped we would find out soon.

Kacie dropped the Eddy questions and latched onto Noah instead. She was ridiculous, practically throwing herself at him. Kacie was just a kinder version of Molly. I wasn't anything like Molly or Kacie.

I thought Noah didn't go for that type of girl. He'd even told me he didn't. But I guess it wasn't true. My personality and my appearance were just not what guys looked for in a girl, at least not Noah. I dragged my feet, letting some distance come between myself and the rest of the group. Being friends with Kacie was exhausting. I just wanted some time alone.

Kacie turned around. "Abby! Come on! We need to hurry or we're going to be late for supper."

I sighed and jogged to catch up. Tyler was waiting for me at the top of the small hill.

"Don't like pizza, huh?" Tyler's eyes twinkled.

I shaded my eyes as I looked up at him. "You just better hope I don't get in line before you."

Tyler cocked his head. "Why's that?"

"Because I'll take whatever's left of the pepperoni," I replied. Even with my hand as sunglasses, I was still squinting.

He grabbed his heart and grimaced. "You're breaking my heart."

I grinned. There was just something about Tyler that made me smile in the midst of my swirling emotions. I wished I had gotten to meet him before Noah. Maybe we could have been more than friends.

Once again, we raced back to the green, slipping into line just in time. If we were going to keep sneaking into the woods, we needed to be a little more careful.

A counselor led us into the dining hall and told us to find our table.

When we opened the door, the director was signaling everyone to be quiet so he could pray. We slid into chairs. Just before I bowed my head, Tyler caught my eye and pretended to wipe the sweat off his brow. A little giggle escaped before I could stop it. He winked and then closed his eyes. I followed suit.

After the prayer, we got in line for our pizza and Tyler made sure he was in front of me. Like I could eat five or six boxes of pepperoni pizza by myself! Apparently, Tyler wasn't going to take any chances.

Kacie sat next to me when we got back to our table. We always beat the boys. They piled food on their plates like it was going to be their last meal ever. "So tell me," she said. "What's really going on between you and Tyler?"

I took a huge bite of pizza, so I wouldn't have to answer.

She leaned her chin on the palm of her hand. "You two are looking pretty tight." She lowered her voice and whispered, "I think he likes you."

I shook my head. "He doesn't like me. Not like that anyway. He's just being nice."

Kacie grinned. "We'll see." She picked up a piece of pizza and took a normal size bite.

Tyler didn't like me, did he? I hoped he didn't because I didn't like him. Not the way Kacie was implying. There weren't any sparks. I didn't get nervous around him like I used to around Noah. Like I still did. No, Tyler and I were just buds. Friends were all we were destined to be. Tyler sat down with his pizza and took a huge bite. He grinned at me from across the table, pizza sauce smeared across his teeth. Gross! I smiled. Definitely just friends. Like I needed more drama this summer.

After dinner was over, we followed Esther back to our cabins. No campfire tonight. Everything was still too wet. Tonight, we were just spending time with the girls.

I sat down Indian style next to Kacie on her bed. We had made a little circle with some girls on the floor and some on the beds.

"Tonight we're just going to share some of the things we've learned so far and, if you're comfortable sharing, some things we're struggling with," Esther said. She tucked her sleek black hair behind her ears. "I'll start. I've learned that forgiveness is something you have to practice everyday because things happen that hurt or annoy you everyday. Something I've been struggling with is trusting God to help me find a job after I'm done being a camp counselor. I graduated from college this spring and just can't seem to find anything. It's a little scary not knowing what I'm going to be doing in a few weeks." She glanced around the circle. "Who would like to go next?"

A couple of girls raised their hand, including Kacie. Esther pointed to the girl sitting next to Kacie.

I tuned out as I thought about what I could share. What had I learned? Nothing I had really wanted to learn. I didn't want to forgive Noah. What he had done to me didn't deserve to be forgiven. As for my struggles, I couldn't talk about being jealous, because Kacie would start asking all kinds of questions I didn't want to answer. So that was out. If I shared that I was crazy angry with someone, then I would get another talk about how important forgiveness was. What could I possibly share? Maybe Esther wouldn't notice if I didn't say anything.

"Abby? Is there anything you would like to share?"

"Uh, sure." I lowered my head and picked at my nail. "I came to camp because my best friend was going to be gone with her parents, and I was feeling lonely. I've learned you can't replace your old friends, but you can definitely make new friends who are just as cool." I put an arm around Kacie and smiled at her.

Kacie beamed.

"Is there anything you've been struggling with?" Esther asked gently.

"Not really. Everything's just peachy." I tried not to grimace as soon as that came out of my mouth. It sounded so fake, but I kept my smile in place.

Esther frowned slightly. "Okay. Thanks for sharing, Abby." She folded her hands. "Well, let's have some fun. I have some games for us to play before it's time for lights out."

She went on to explain the games, and I sighed in relief.

Kacie whispered, "I feel the same about you. I'm so glad we met." She squeezed my hand and then turned her attention back to Esther.

I could feel the guilt weighing on my shoulders. If only Kacie didn't have a major crush on Noah. Then maybe I could have meant what I said. Sometimes, Kacie was my friend, and sometimes Kacie was my enemy. I had just made my first frenemy. And the worst part was, she didn't even know.

DUCK!

"Finally we get some pool time," Kacie said. Her pink-and-white striped towel was tucked under her arm. "I want a tan so bad."

I looked at her already browned skin and then at the white skin on my arm, just a shade above pasty. "Me too." I frowned. The sun just didn't like me.

"Think Noah will like my swimsuit?" Kacie asked with an anxious look on her face.

I didn't have to glance at her baby blue one piece with matching cover-up to know he would. Another thing she owned that wasn't pink. That made two. Kacie's swimsuit was so cute it made me wish I had bought a new suit to wear instead of my faded red one. "I'm sure he will. But why do you care, anyway? Noah's a jerk. I mean, stinkbugs in my hair?"

Kacie wrinkled her nose. "He apologized for that. Besides, it was probably Tyler's idea too."

"Well, it was still rude," I said matter-of-factly.

Kacie changed the subject. "I don't even want to get in the pool today. If I get my hair wet, it'll be a frizzy mess later. I would just die if Noah saw me like that."

"I can't wait to get in! The water will feel awesome!" There was silence for a second, filled only with the slap of our flip-flops on the worn path. "Besides, Tyler said there's a volleyball net, and he challenged me to a game."

A slow smile grew on Kacie's face. "Well, you don't want to miss that."

I rolled my eyes. "Just friends, Kace, just friends."

We walked up to the pool area and opened the gate. Kacie took her time picking out a lounger sitting fully in the bright sun. She carefully laid her towel out while I dumped my stuff next to her.

"Hi, ladies! Come on in," Tyler yelled from the deep end. Just his head stuck out of the water, his brown hair every-which-way.

Kacie shook her head. "Tanning!"

I shed my old knit shorts and walked to the edge of the pool. Tyler rested his hands on the side.

"Too chicken to get in, too?" Tyler asked, a goofy grin on his face.

Without warning, I jumped in, hoping my splash would drench him. When I resurfaced, I could hear Tyler's laughter. I wiped the water from my face while trying to keep myself afloat. "Still think I'm chicken?"

Tyler smacked me on the back. I tried not to wince as I lurched forward from the impact. "Nope. Let's get this game started."

We swam over to the volleyball net, Tyler ducked under, and he grabbed the volleyball floating nearby.

"You know you're going to get crushed," Tyler said, tossing the yellow ball back and forth between his hands.

I studied his towering frame through the net. "I think we should make a no spiking rule."

"What! No. Then it won't be a true game." He floated the ball in the water in front of him.

"It won't be fair otherwise, because you can spike, but I can't. I'm way shorter than you!" Sure the net wasn't *that* high, but he still had a definite advantage over me.

Tyler held up his hands. "Okay, okay. No spiking it is. Ready?"

I took a deep breath, backed up a little, and got in my stance. "Yup."

Tyler didn't have to jump to hit the ball after he tossed it in the air. He smacked the ball over the net. I bumped it back. He reached and bumped it back over. I sent the ball sailing back over the net. Tyler reached up easily with one hand and smacked it over, but it went to the left and hit the concrete.

"Who's going to get crushed?" I asked, grinning.

Tyler looked impressed. "I may have underestimated you."

"Can I play?" Noah asked, dog-paddling over to us.

"Sure," Tyler said easily. "You can be on my team."

"Now, wait a second." I put my hands on my hips. "If you get a partner, I get a partner."

"Kace!" Tyler yelled. "Come play! Abby needs help! And can you get our ball before you get in?"

Kacie didn't even open her eyes. "I'll get your ball, but I'm not playing. There's some serious tanning going on here." She stood up, grabbed the ball that had rolled not far from her lounger, and tossed it back in the pool.

I squeezed my eyes shut as the ball splashed water in my face. "You're not going to let these guys gang up on me, are you?"

"It'll be fun, Kacie," Noah said.

She hesitated a minute before heading toward the stairs. "Okay, but no one can splash my face."

Was she serious? We were in a pool.

Kacie backed down the stairs, flinching when the cold water hit her legs. "This is freezing!"

"It'll warm up. Come on. It's our serve," I said. I tossed the ball up in the air and caught it.

She walked on tiptoes toward the net; her arms raised so they wouldn't touch the water. "I should probably tell you I'm not so good at this game."

I knew I was going to need a real teammate, so I glanced around the pool, and then yelled, "Dylan!"

Dylan turned, smiled, and swam over. "Hey, guys."

"I didn't know your group was in the pool too," Tyler said. He smacked Dylan on the back.

"I am in serious need of another teammate," I said.

"Hey!" Kacie said, still on her tiptoes.

I shot her a look. "Like I said, I desperately need a partner."

Dylan's face lit up. "Really? I'll play!"

"Two against three? Not fair, Abby," Noah said.

I pointed at Kacie. "You're afraid of her?"

Noah backed off without saying another word.

"Do you want to serve first?" I asked Dylan.

Dylan moved toward the net. "No, you can."

I tossed the ball up, jumped, and whacked it across the net.

Noah easily returned it, and I sent it back to him. He hit it again, and it sailed toward Kacie. Kacie watched it land on the water next to her.

"Kacie! That was right to you!" I said, throwing my hands in the air.

"I told you I wasn't good at this game." Kacie reached up and smoothed her hair.

I sighed and heaved the ball back to the boys. "Your serve." Hopefully, Dylan would at least try to hit the ball.

Noah bounced back to his serving position.

Tyler grinned. "You've got this, Noah. Easy point."

I stuck my tongue out at Tyler and readied myself for Noah's serve.

Tyler and Noah were a good team, and I wouldn't have had a chance with just Kacie as my teammate. Fortunately, Dylan was pretty good. He was good enough that we battled for the lead, but then Noah and Tyler pulled ahead. I decided to call for one last shot before the game got out of control.

"The almighty Abby is giving up?" Noah asked. He gave Tyler a high-five.

I pointed at Kacie shivering in the water. "She's freezing."

"Just an excuse," Noah said. "You don't want to admit you're not any good."

The spark in Noah's blue eyes fired me up. "Just serve the ball," I said through clenched teeth. Not good, huh? This was one shot he wasn't going to forget.

Noah served and the ball glided over the net. I jumped as high as I could out of the water, my arm raised. If I aimed right, the ball would just barely miss Noah's face. I smacked the ball so hard that my palm stung. As I landed, I watched the ball hit Noah right above his left eye with a loud thud. He looked stunned.

I was shocked at my miscalculation. The ball wasn't supposed to hit him in the face.

Kacie pushed through the water, ducked under the net, and went straight to Noah. "Are you okay?"

"You could have really hurt him," Tyler said softly.

I rubbed my sore hand. "He shouldn't have been picking on me."

Tyler's brown eyes stared straight into mine. "That doesn't mean you go for a head shot."

It didn't look like he would believe the truth, so I tried to save face. "You have to admit it was a great shot." I crossed my arms.

Tyler shook his head. "Sorry, Abs, but that was just plain mean." He made his way toward Noah, Kacie, and Dylan. "I bet you get a shiner, dude."

I didn't join them, instead trying to ignore the sting of Tyler's words. It had been an accident, not that Noah hadn't deserved it, but I would never have done something like that on purpose. Tyler didn't know what he was talking about.

By the time I was done reflecting, Kacie, Tyler, and Dylan had helped Noah out of the pool. A lifeguard was asking him questions to make sure he didn't have a concussion or anything. I thought they were being a little excessive. The ball hadn't hit him that hard.

Using the ladder, I climbed out of the pool and grabbed my towel to dry off. Kacie joined me.

"You need to go apologize to Noah," Kacie told me, hands on her hips. "You hurt him."

"He's fine." I dried my legs and started on my arms.

"I don't care. You keep telling me how rude he is, but the only rude person I see is you. Apologize. Now." Kacie tapped her right foot, hands still on her hips.

"No." Kacie was not my mother, and I certainly wasn't going to let her bully me. I turned my back on her and slid my shorts back on. "If anyone needs me, I'll be on the other side of the pool." When I looked back at Kacie, her mouth was hanging open, her eyes wide. I was steamed. Apologize! To Noah? Sorry, but that was not going to happen. Not in a million years.

It wasn't fair that everyone had turned against me, I thought as I stomped away. Noah was the jerk. Not me. I didn't understand why Kacie and Tyler were on his side. Hot tears slid down my cheeks. If they knew what Noah had done, they wouldn't be having a pity party for him. The minute I saw him at this camp, I should have insisted I wasn't staying—thrown a temper tantrum, screamed, cried, anything to keep my parents from leaving me here. I was never talking to my parents or Kacie and Tyler again, and especially not Noah.

I dropped into a lounge chair and closed my eyes, hoping that would keep tears from spilling out.

"Abby?"

Opening my eyes a tiny bit, I saw Esther in the chair next to me.

"Why don't you tell me what happened."

I shut my eyes again. "Why? I'm sure you already heard Kacie's version."

"Can I hear your version?" Esther asked, her voice as soft as my sheets back home.

I wanted to be at home so badly right now. Where was Claire when I needed her?

"Please?"

I sighed. "Noah was picking on me. I just wanted to show him how good I am." I stopped to get control of my emotions. "I didn't mean to hit him in the face. It was an accident." I sniffled.

Esther patted my arm. "I believe you." She stood up. "Let's go apologize to Noah and get this whole thing cleared up."

I thought I heard her wrong. "Apologize?"

"That's what you do when an accident happens," Esther said. She grabbed my hand and pulled me up. "I'll go with you."

I was hopping mad. Why didn't Noah have to apologize to me? He was just as guilty as I was.

Esther stopped right in front of Noah. Someone had given him an ice pack, which he was holding over his eye. "Abby has something to say. Abby?"

I glared at the ground. "I didn't hit you on purpose. It was an accident. I'm sorry." When I looked up, Kacie had a triumphant smile on her face. I was right. She was exactly like Molly.

"Thank you, Abby," Esther said. "Noah, do you have anything to say?"

I smiled. Esther was making him apologize too.

Noah lowered his ice pack giving me a full view of his battered eye. "I accept your apology, Abby. I know you didn't mean to hurt me."

My mouth dropped open. That was all he had to say?

"Wonderful," Esther said. "Now let's gather our things and head back to the cabin to change." Esther called to the rest of the girls.

I was so angry I couldn't see straight. When we arrived back at the cabin, I quickly changed out of my wet swimsuit and into dry clothes. I climbed up to my bed and curled up in my sleeping bag. If Esther thought everything had been taken care of with that apology she was wrong. I was angrier at Noah now than when I had come to this stupid camp. And now that anger included Kacie too.

I missed Claire so much. Claire always knew the right thing to say, and she always stuck up for me. Why couldn't Kacie be more like Claire? Kacie was just as vicious as Molly. I hated that smirk on her face when Esther made me apologize to Noah, like she was a perfect princess. Well, she wasn't. Kacie wasn't a princess and she definitely wasn't my friend.

PIECE OF THE PUZZLE

THE NEXT MORNING, I was feeling pretty proud of myself for avoiding the three musketeers as I was now calling them, but I knew I couldn't avoid them forever. I tried to be the first of the girls to sit down at breakfast but still ended up next to Kacie. I sat down and didn't make eye contact with her or the boys.

After the prayer, I dawdled up to the line, but still managed to be right behind Kacie. When Kacie reached the plates, she grabbed two, turned, smiled, and gave me one. "I'm sorry about yesterday. I was just really scared that Noah was hurt bad."

Kacie's smile and apology surprised me. I had no idea what to say. "Okay."

She held out her hand. "Friends?"

I stared at her hand like I'd never seen one before. Yesterday, she'd been all up in my face and then tattled to Esther and now we were supposed to be friends?

Right. I ignored her hand. "Sure." She was definitely a frenemy.

Kacie hesitated and then lowered her hand.

I guess I was supposed to be incredibly grateful she still wanted to be my friend. Whatever. "Thanks for the plate." I waved it in the air.

Kacie's smile returned in full force. "You're welcome."

I filled my plate with scrambled eggs and bacon and returned to the table right behind Kacie. As I sat down, I heard a deep voice whisper in my ear.

"We need to sneak into the woods again. We're running out of time," Dylan said. "Tomorrow, during free time." He scurried off.

Dylan's urgency made me feel like a spy in some novel, so when Tyler asked what Dylan wanted, I forgot I was mad at him. "He wants us to meet him tomorrow to search."

"I'm not sure we should," Tyler said.

"Me either," Noah said. "I'm sorry about his cousin, but we could get in big trouble."

I looked up at Noah and winced. His eye was a mess. Dark blue and purple splotches marked the area.

"Noah's right," Kacie said.

I dropped my fork, taking pleasure in the clatter it made when it hit my tray. "Well, I'm going. The three of you can stick together. Whatever. But Dylan is my friend, and I'm helping him." I got up to dump my tray. Suddenly, I wasn't hungry anymore.

When I returned to the table, I put my head down. I had no desire to talk to any of them.

Kacie put her head next to mine. "We decided to go too."

"Fantastic." I didn't even try to keep the sarcasm out of my voice.

"Noah said you were right. He said we should stick with our friends. All of them," Kacie said.

I lifted my head to look at Noah. He and Tyler were arm wrestling. Noah had really said that?

Kacie grinned. "I have a feeling we'll solve the case tomorrow."

All day I had to listen to Kacie's speculations about what we'd find on our hunt for clues. She wasn't sure she would be able to sleep with so much adventure awaiting us tomorrow. That was funny since she hadn't wanted to go in the first place. I just wanted to knock myself out so I wouldn't have to listen to her any more.

Free time the next day couldn't come fast enough. I wanted to get searching and away from Kacie.

Kacie and I were the first to sneak away. While we waited for the boys at the pond, I used the elastic hair band on my wrist to pull my hair up into a sloppy bun. Tramping around in the woods with my hair down was just asking for trouble. Wishing for a mirror, I felt for any bubbles on top of my head.

"Don't worry. Tyler will think you look cute." Kacie giggled. She was pulling her hair up too.

I didn't bother trying to correct her. Let her think what she wanted.

The boys finally joined us.

"Okay, Dylan, take the lead," Tyler said.

Dylan stepped into the woods and led us back toward the boys' cabins. "I think we should look here."

Tyler nodded. "Sure."

"Let's go straight back and then spread out," I said.

Dylan again took the lead, and I lagged behind the others.

Tyler hung back with me. "I wanted to apologize for yesterday. I was kind of harsh."

"Kind of?" I asked.

He held up his hands. "Fine, fine. A lot harsh."

I noticed Tyler repeated words a lot. It was kind of cute.

"Anyway, I really am sorry." Tyler laid his hand on my arm.

I shoved him. "Sure you are. You're just happy I convinced you to be a detective again."

Tyler grinned. "Well, there is that."

I shoved him again and he laughed. When we caught up to the others, they were standing beneath a ginormous tree with huge roots, sticking out of the ground.

I ran my hands over the tree's bark, wondering how old it was.

Tyler stared straight up. "This is one massive tree."

Kacie and Noah also stared amazed at the tree.

"Gosh! I can't even imagine what the redwoods in California look like if they're bigger than this!" Kacie said.

"I think we should start looking here," Dylan said, getting us back on mission.

Noah and Tyler wiped sweat off their foreheads with their tee shirt sleeves. It was getting hot. I was positive my hair was frizzier than frizzy. Of course, Kacie still looked fabulous despite the heat.

I screwed up my lips and wrinkled my nose. "We don't have a lot of time."

"Then, let's start looking," Dylan said. He strode over to a piece of dead bark and knelt down.

"I still don't really know what to look for," Noah said.

Kacie lightly punched him on the arm. "For clues, silly."

"Something else like the hat would be cool," Tyler said.

We all grew quiet as we searched in bushes, under leaves, and in tree trunks. Several minutes of searching led to nothing.

"We can't stay much longer," I said. "Free time has to be ending soon."

Dylan was frantic. "Just a few more minutes."

We went back to searching.

I was just about to tell everyone I was going back, when Dylan started hooting and hollering. "Look! Look!"

I jogged to Dylan's side and knelt next to him. The others crowded around.

"I found this under the bush!" Dylan cradled a picture. It was a faded school picture of a girl about our age. She was pretty—red hair, blue eyes, freckles. I took the picture from Dylan and flipped it over. Goosebumps covered my arms when I saw Darcy's name written in purple flowery writing.

"Is that really Darcy?" Kacie asked in a hushed voice.

I flipped the picture back over to Darcy's smiling face.

Dylan nodded. "I met her once. At a family thing."

"Eddy was here." I could barely breathe.

Noah straightened. "We need to go or we're going to get caught."

Dylan pocketed the picture.

As we hiked back, Dylan asked us again not to share this with anyone else.

"I really think we should tell a counselor, Dyl," Tyler said. "This is getting serious."

"Just think about how spooked everyone would be," Dylan said. "And police would be everywhere."

I was already spooked, and I knew Kacie was too.

The arguments continued, but Dylan finally convinced us to keep everything quiet. It was his cousin—his mystery to solve.

"Do you think we'll go out again?" Kacie whispered as we left the woods.

"I don't know. I'm sure soon," I said.

Kacie nodded. "Poor Eddy."

Poor Eddy indeed. I shivered. What really had happened to Eddy?

LOVE OR REVENGE

THE NEXT DAY, I was still thinking about the volleyball incident. Hitting Noah with the volleyball had been a huge mistake, and I felt a little bothered by the fact that I still didn't feel very sorry about it. I had given Noah a black eye. I should feel really bad, but mostly what I felt was anger that everyone had taken Noah's side. I didn't understand why everyone felt so bad for Noah all the time, but never for me.

I still needed to come up with a prank to get Noah back for the pond muck. My brother had done a prank at camp that was awesome if I could pull it off. This prank would be way better than hiding a pile of stinky pond scum under the bed. I'd have to sneak off by myself while everyone else was busy. It shouldn't be too hard. Sneaking into the woods had been a piece of cake.

This afternoon's activity was archery. I was pretty excited about shooting arrows. I was going to be way better at this than ceramics. Kacie, however, was nervous about it.

"I don't understand why you actually want to do archery," Kacie said. "It's so dangerous."

"Kace, we're not shooting at anything but targets." I tightened my ponytail and put my brush back in my suitcase. "Just relax."

She stuck out her bottom lip. "How can I relax when I know someone could get hurt?"

"Didn't you read the brochure before you got here?" I asked, knowing she had. She practically had the brochure memorized.

"Yes." She grabbed her brush and ran it through her curly hair. Each curl bounced back into its coil after the brush passed through it.

"Well, then I'm sure you knew archery was a part of camp." I plopped down on her bed.

Kacie's brush paused in her hair as she thought. "I forgot about it."

"They wouldn't let us do this if it was dangerous," I said. "You'll have fun, I bet."

"You just don't understand," Kacie said. She lifted her nose in the air.

"Seriously, Kace? You're acting a little crazy right now." Under my breath I muttered, "As usual."

"What? What did you just say?" Kacie asked, pointing her brush at me like a sword.

"Nothing." I held my hands, palms out, in front of me. I could see the headline now. Abby Rivers: Death by Hairbrush. "All I'm saying is maybe you shouldn't be so upset about something that's supposed to be fun.

I don't like ceramics, but you didn't hear me whining about it."

That silenced her. I wasn't about to let cute, always-get-my-way Kacie ruin my archery day. I was pretty sure I would be able to show the boys up when it came to this activity.

Kacie continued to give me the silent treatment, even after we met up with the boys.

"What's up with her?" Tyler asked me after he said hi to Kacie and she swept past him without saying a word.

"She's mad I'm not taking her side about archery being the greatest evil known to man," I told him. "Don't worry. She'll get over it."

Tyler glanced over to where Noah was standing and grinned. "I think I'm glad I'm over here."

When I looked, I saw Kacie's mouth going a mile a minute. Apparently, Noah was getting her whole lecture about archery being dangerous. I grinned too. Standing next to Tyler was the best place to be right now.

"So, how many bull's-eyes do you think you can get?" Tyler asked, his eyes twinkling.

I lifted my shoulder in a half shrug. "I don't know."

"Want to make a wager?" Tyler asked.

"No, thanks. I don't want to get involved with whatever it is you have planned."

"So you don't even want to hear the bet?" Tyler asked. "It's good." He waggled his eyebrows.

He was baiting me for sure, and it worked. I was too curious to let him walk away without explaining. "Wait.

Let's say I was interested in challenging you, not that I am, but what would the bet be?"

Tyler leaned down toward me with a grin on his face. "If I get the least number of bull's-eyes, then I have to ask you to the camp dance. If you get the least number of bull's-eyes, you have to eat a worm."

I could feel my eyes widen as my pulse kicked up. "What?"

"You heard me," Tyler whispered. He walked away, but before he was out of earshot, he turned and called, "Let me know if you're interested!"

Was he serious? Part of me wanted to say yes. At least I'd have a date for the dance because I would beat him. Part of me wanted to wait to see if Noah would ask me. I knew it was weird to be so angry at him, and at the same time to want him to ask me to the dance, but I couldn't help it. He hadn't asked Kacie yet, so maybe he would ask me. I watched Kacie and Noah chatting and laughing. Who was I kidding? Noah was just taking his good old sweet time asking her. I should take Tyler's bet. Eating a slimy worm was definitely not something I wanted to do, but I would beat Tyler. Archery was going to be my thing.

I walked over to Tyler who was leaning against a tree, chewing on a piece of grass, and reached up to tap him on the shoulder. "You're on."

Tyler's smile stretched across his face. "Want ketchup for your worm? Maybe some barbeque sauce?"

"Who says I'm going to lose?" I put my hands on my hips. Boys always thought they were better than girls. So annoying.

"I do. I know how good I am." Tyler followed the other kids as they started walking.

Ugh! I hurried to catch up.

When we arrived at the archery station, Tyler sat next to me so we could get neighboring targets. He said it was so he could make sure I didn't cheat. Like I would need to.

Chad and Esther gave us a demonstration of how to line up your bow and shoot the arrow on target. Then they let us loose to find arm protectors and to start shooting.

When Tyler and I were banded and at our targets, properly armed, Tyler asked, "Are you ready for this?"

"I was born ready," I replied. A cheesy line, I knew, but I couldn't help it. I was going to win this bet.

Tyler pulled the string back and let his arrow fly. It struck the target slightly off the bull's-eye.

I narrowed my eyes. "Am I missing something?"

Tyler grinned. "Didn't I mention that my grandpa taught me how to shoot when I was like five?"

Inwardly, I groaned. "No, you failed to tell me that. How come I think that was on purpose?"

Tyler didn't answer. He shot again, this time getting a perfect bull's-eye. "How good are you?"

"Guess we'll find out." I turned toward the target, now nervous, especially since I knew Tyler was watching me. I set my feet. My fingers trembled as I pulled the string back. I let my arrow fly and completely missed the target.

Tyler threw his head back and laughed loudly. "Looks like I have this one in the bag."

I bit my lip. No way was I going to miss the target again. I armed myself, pulled the string, and let go. This time my arrow found a mark. Not a bull's-eye, but a whole lot closer.

"Keep trying, Rivers," Tyler said. "Maybe you'll be able to catch up."

Out of the corner of my eye, I could see him hit another bull's-eye. "You tricked me."

Tyler chuckled. "All right. In fairness, I won't count those two. That was just my warm-up."

That was sort of fair. When Chad and Esther came this way, they would be able to help me adjust my stance. Then maybe it would be a little more even. In the meantime, I just needed to concentrate.

I kept trying, over and over until my arrow was a hair away from the bull's-eye. Before I could break concentration, I put another arrow in, aimed, and let it soar. Bull's-eye!

"Beginner's luck. Won't happen again," Tyler said, as he came back from retrieving his arrows.

"Thanks for the encouragement." After several more shots, I began to relax. I was pretty good at this, beginner's luck or not.

At the end of the session, we were all tied up at three.

"Looks like we'll never know who won," I said, unstrapping my arm band.

"Technically, I won, because your target is closer than mine," Tyler said.

I slung my bow over my shoulder. "You didn't make any rules about distance." I restrapped my armband. "Tiebreak shot?"

By this time, Noah and Kacie had joined us.

"What's going on?" Kacie asked. She didn't have a bow but she was still wearing her armband. Of course she'd managed to find a pink one.

"Tyler's too chicken to truly test his skill out on a rookie like me," I said, staring him down.

He considered for a minute and then nodded his head. "Okay, but what if we both miss?"

"If neither of us gets a bull's-eye, then whoever's closer wins. Still game?" I grabbed an arrow because I knew he would be.

"What does the winner get?" Noah asked.

"That's between me and Abby." Tyler picked up an arrow. "Who's going first?"

"You. And hurry, because we're the last ones." I wanted to see how well he did so I would know what I had to do to win. I always worked better under pressure.

Tyler got ready, hesitated, and then let go. His arrow stuck just a hair off the bull's-eye. "Beat that, Abs!"

I readied my arrow, took a deep breath, aimed, and let go. I squeezed my eyes shut, not sure I wanted to see the results. When no one said anything, I opened them. A perfect bull's-eye. I let the grin come. "I'm just going to collect my arrows."

I could hear Tyler's feet crunching in the grass next to me. When I stopped, he went a little further to his target.

Tyler bent over to pick his arrows. "Admit it. You knew how to do this before you came."

"Nope. I promise. Just natural ability." I couldn't hide my smile.

Tyler stood up, his hand full of arrows. "Well, I have a question for you."

"I wonder what it is." I picked up my last arrow and then rested a hand on my hip. "I don't know how I feel about you asking me to the dance because you lost a bet. Somehow, it doesn't seem very romantic."

"It doesn't, does it?" An attractive smile crossed his tanned face. "Maybe I shouldn't ask you."

I smacked his shoulder. "Backing out of your own bet?"

Tyler shook his head. "Nope." His grin widened. "You really think I couldn't have hit that bull's-eye?"

I could feel my face get hot. Did he mean what I thought he did? I shaded my eyes with my hand as I looked up at him. "You lost on purpose?"

His smile didn't falter. "So, go to the dance with me?"

My mind flicked to an image of Noah, but I knew in my heart he wouldn't ask me. Kacie had snagged him the first day of camp. "Yes."

"Awesome." He turned around to head back to the shooting area. "Let's get our stuff put away. Everybody watching us is kind of creeping me out."

I nodded and followed him.

As we were putting our gear away, Chad asked, "So who won?"

Tyler winked at me. "I did."

I could feel my face heat up again. I didn't know what to say.

Back at the cabin, Kacie asked me what Tyler had to do since he lost.

I didn't want to tell her because I knew she would gloat, but she'd find out sooner or later. "He's taking me to the dance."

Kacie squealed, clapped her hands, and leaned over to give me a monster hug. "I'm so excited for you! Noah will ask me and then everything will be perfect!" She went back to the letter she was writing, her pen flying across the paper.

I slumped against the wall of Kacie's bed. Nothing was perfect at all. I was trying hard to hide the heartbreak I felt for not being Noah's choice for the dance. Again. I didn't care why Tyler had asked me. I was just glad someone had. At least I wouldn't be sitting on the sidelines forced to watch the Kacie and Noah love story.

At supper that night, Kacie and Tyler laughed and chatted, but I wasn't in the mood. I tried to laugh at Tyler's corny jokes, but my heart wasn't in it. Noah was quiet too. Even Kacie couldn't get him to talk, and she most definitely tried. She kept throwing me helpless glances. I didn't know what I was supposed to do about it. She was way closer to him than I was these days.

Finally, Tyler clapped Noah on the back. "What's going on, dude?"

Noah swirled his glass of milk and grunted.

"We just want to help," Kacie said, laying her hand on Noah's arm. "Are you sick, or did you get some bad news?"

"You could say that," Noah muttered just loud enough for us to hear. He raised his head. "I don't want to talk about it, okay?"

Kacie jerked her hand back like she'd been stung. Apparently, she'd never been snapped at before. "Sorry. I didn't mean to annoy you."

Noah softened his tone. "It's okay. I just really don't want to talk about it." He took a swig of his milk.

Kacie nodded, but you could tell she didn't quite understand. She was the kind of girl who talked through all her problems and probably shared those problems with anyone who would listen.

Tyler set his fork down. "Well, I'm ready for campfire tonight." He turned to me. "Abs, are you going to be my campfire buddy?"

My face felt hot as I quickly became the center of attention. "Sure, as long as you bring you-know-what."

Tyler grinned and answered with a chipper, "You bet."

I sat through the campfire with Tyler, not listening at all to what was going on. Doubts kept running through my head. Maybe going to the dance with Tyler wasn't the right thing to do. Noah might have asked me. I wavered between crushing on him and hating him. I couldn't decide what I wanted, love or revenge. Then I remembered that moment with Molly when my whole world had come crashing down. I remembered a dozen different times when he and Kacie were flirting and making goo-goo eyes at each other. I picked revenge.

That night, after all the girls in the cabin were asleep, I snuck out. I went straight to the boys' row of cabins and found the cabin I wanted, 14B. As silently as I could, I climbed the two wooden steps up to the porch, put my ear to the door to listen for any voices, and heard none. Slowly, I opened the screen door so it wouldn't squeak. I could feel my heart beating fast and tried to calm myself down. Breaking into the boys' cabin couldn't be a more serious offense than being in the woods without a counselor. I slipped through the door and was careful not to let it bang behind me. I kept my flashlight pointed at the floor so I wouldn't wake anyone with its light. Then, I set every alarm clock in the cabin to a different time. If I planned it right, the boys would be up every half hour.

After slipping back out undetected, I let a smile cross my face. I snuck back into my cabin and into bed. It took forever to fall asleep because I couldn't wait to see those tired faces in the morning. If it worked, I was pretty sure my excited face would tell them exactly who'd done it.

SURVIVING

THE NEXT MORNING, I was very impatient to get to the dining hall. "Your hair looks fine," I told Kacie for the twentieth time.

She fluffed her hair again and checked it in her mirror. "I don't know. Noah hasn't asked me to the dance yet, and something was really up with him last night."

It was a little weird Noah hadn't asked Kacie yet, but he would. Typical boy, he just hadn't gotten around to it yet. My brother didn't ask his girlfriend to prom until the day before. It was a good thing she'd already bought a dress. "I'm pretty sure it's not because of your hair," I said.

Kacie gave me a sharp glance. "What is that supposed to mean?"

Yikes! She was really defensive. "It means he just hasn't thought about it yet."

She sighed and put the mirror down. "I guess you're right. It's just that Tyler asked you."

"The difference is Tyler and I are just friends and you and Noah"—it hurt to say this—"look more like boyfriend-girlfriend to me."

"You think so?" Kacie's eyes were filled with hope.

I wanted to be wrong. Oh, how I hoped I was wrong. "Yes, but remember he's not the nicest of guys," I said, sitting on Kacie's bed, watching her put her stuff away. "Moody, impatient, rude." I checked them off on my fingers.

Kacie snapped her suitcase closed. "You're wrong about Noah. He's perfect." Her face took on this dreamy look that I didn't want to watch at all.

"I'm getting in line for breakfast," I said, standing up. I was not wasting another minute watching Kacie primp and preen for Noah. I wanted to revel in the victory of my perfect prank, which I could only do at the dining hall. Of course, I would have to revel in secret.

Finally, we made it to breakfast and my first glimpse of the boys made me want to laugh out loud. All the boys were either laying their heads on the table or leaning their heads against their hands. All of them had their eyes closed. Tyler was out cold, a thin trail of drool slipping down his chin. I was going to enjoy this.

I sat down and slammed my hands on the table. Heads jerked up. Even some of the girls seating themselves squealed in surprise. "Morning!"

Kacie looked at me like I was a bug to be squashed. "That wasn't very nice."

"It's almost time for prayer anyway," I said.

"What's wrong with you guys? Did you stay up all night?" Kacie asked Tyler.

Tyler yawned. "Someone set our alarms at all different times. I swear we were up every fifteen minutes."

"That's genius!" I said, hoping I would throw them off. I needed to keep a low profile on this one. "Wish I would have thought of that."

"So you didn't do it," Noah said, sounding like he didn't believe me. He rubbed his right eye but didn't touch his left one. It was still puffy, although now it was more yellow and green than purple and blue.

I tried to make my face look surprised. "How would I have done that? Sounds like an inside job to me."

Noah's eyes narrowed. "I don't believe you."

I shrugged. "Whatever."

Our conversation was cut short by the director asking us to bow our heads and it was never picked up again, even after we all had our food and were reseated. I had gotten away with it!

Today's activity was survival huts. It sounded like fun. You never knew when you were going to get stranded in the woods, like Eddy had.

Just as I had that thought, Kacie brought Eddy up. "We'll be out in the woods again today, so we should look for Eddy clues." She twirled a curl around her finger.

I was a little spooked after our last adventure with Dylan, so I wasn't in a hurry to find anything else. "I just want to learn about survival huts."

"But there's a missing person out there!" Kacie said, dropping her curl. "Don't you want to be a part of finding him?"

"Not really," I said. "Besides, if he was going to be found, the police would have already found him. I'm sure they brought dogs and everything out here. A whole search and rescue team." I scuffed my shoe in the grass. Why weren't we leaving? I looked around, hoping to see Esther or Chad ready to go.

"They could have missed something"—Kacie pointed her finger at me—"we can't let Eddy down."

I rolled my eyes.

"Well, if you won't help me, Noah will." Kacie crossed her arms and stuck her bottom lip out in a pout. While it was a ridiculous look on most people above the age of five, on Kacie, it looked adorable. Of course.

"What will I help with?" Noah asked.

Kacie brightened up. "Searching for Eddy."

"I don't know, Kace," Noah replied. "I don't think I want to stumble onto Eddy."

Tyler nodded. "I think we should convince Dylan to give everything we found to the police."

I grinned. Finally the boys were on my side.

Kacie brought out her pouty face once again. "Well, I'm going to look, even if you guys don't."

Esther clapped her hands to get everyone's attention. "All right, guys. Today we're going to go off the trail a bit to make our survival huts. Please stick together while in the woods so we don't lose anyone."

"We'll be working in two-person teams today," Chad said. "So pick a partner. This person will also be your partner in the woods, so you can keep track of each other."

Kacie looped her arm through mine. I was surprised she didn't pick Noah.

Tyler had a mischievous twinkle in his eye that signaled trouble. "I bet Noah and I can build our hut faster and better than yours."

"I bet not," I said.

"We'll see about that." Tyler turned to follow the campers into the woods, a little bounce in his step.

Kacie grinned. "You guys are so cute!"

I ignored her.

When we got to our destination, Chad and Esther gave us a tutorial on how to make different kinds of survival huts. Kacie and I decided on the teepee kind. We thought it would be easier and faster. Anything to beat the boys!

"You can go into the woods to find anything you would like to build your huts. Just stay within yelling distance, and watch out for poison ivy," Chad said. "Build away!"

We began by looking for a good spot for our survival hut. Our campmates were also scouting out good areas, so we had to be fast, especially if we wanted to beat the guys. Kacie quickly found two trees whose trunks were close together. She guarded our site, picking up smaller twigs to use for the outside while I searched for larger things to provide the frame. It took us a long time to support the longer branches against the tree. They kept slipping off, but finally, an hour later, we had a pretty decent hut. I stood back to admire our work while Kacie kept finding leaves and twigs to fill in the holes.

When we had finished, we wandered over to check out Tyler and Noah's creation.

I have to admit I was a little in awe of what they had built. They had chosen to do a debris hut, so they had a long piece of wood anchored in the fork of a tree, slanted down to the ground. Then they had leaned other large limbs against the long piece, with leaves, twigs, and whatever else they could find to cover it. We might have gotten done faster, but theirs was much better.

Kacie was speechless. Something she hadn't been since I'd met her.

"This is awesome," I finally said.

Tyler looked up from where he was still filling holes. He frowned. "You guys done?"

I nodded. "But you win, hands down."

Kacie agreed. "Ours isn't anything like this."

Noah poked his head out from inside the hut. "It looks good in here, Tyler." He saw us and grinned. "Pretty cool, huh?"

There would be no stopping their bragging now.

"It's awesome," Kacie said, still inspecting it. "Can I check out the inside?"

"Sure," Noah said. "Come on in."

"What does yours look like?" Tyler asked. He put down a handful of leaves and brushed his hands off.

"Pretty much like all the other huts our group built." Everyone, except for Tyler and Noah, had chosen to do the teepee style.

"I think you guys get the blue ribbon today," Chad said, interrupting Tyler's conversation with me. "This is cool. It might be the best one the camp has seen so far!"

Tyler grinned. "We shoot for the stars!" Only goofy Tyler would say something that lame.

Chad leisurely checked the hut out, poking at things and examining spots. "Yup, this is a solid hut. Awesome job."

As Chad walked away to help others, Noah and Kacie crawled out. Kacie made a beeline for me.

"What's the inside look like?" I kind of wanted to see it too.

Kacie's face was about the same color as her bright pink shorts. "Guess what?" she asked, completely ignoring my question.

"What?" I was only half focused on her, still thinking about the inside of their hut.

"Noah just asked me to the dance," Kacie said, and I felt like I'd been punched in the stomach.

I tried to summon up any happy feelings for Kacie, but couldn't. Not even a smile. "That's great," I muttered.

Kacie was too much in her happy bubble to notice my lack of enthusiasm. "He just kind of blurted it out," she whispered. "I think he was nervous."

I remembered another time when Noah had been nervous, and I tried not to cry. Crying would be bad right now. I blinked faster, imagining my eyelids as windshield wipers clearing the rain.

"Are you okay?" Kacie asked, now noticing my distress.

I rubbed my eyes. "I think I got some dust or something in my eyes."

"I'm sorry," she said and then moved on. "This is so perfect! You and Tyler, and me and Noah. It's going to be so much fun!" Kacie was grinning like she'd won the Miss America title or something.

Fun? That's not the word I would use. Nightmarish. Torturous. Those are the words that came to my mind. I wasn't sure I could survive this again. Sure I had known it was coming, but it still felt unexpected, and so painful. With the pain came anger, hot and fierce. Noah would pay.

Chad and Esther took pictures of everyone's survival huts and then we were headed back to camp.

I barely touched my food at lunch. Everything tasted like cardboard. I wished Claire was here. Her sarcasm and understanding would be amazing right now. Why did she have to abandon me for Europe?

During free time, we congregated at the edge of the green to decide what to do about Dylan.

That was when we noticed a lone figure pulling a suitcase across the green. He was noticeably short.

"Is that Dylan?" Kacie asked.

We went over to meet him. He looked awful.

"What's going on, Dyl?" Tyler asked.

He studied his zebra shoes. "I'm going home." He paused and then said, "I got caught in the woods this morning."

I gasped. Had he ratted us out?

"Don't worry. I didn't say anything about you guys," Dylan said quickly.

"What were you doing in the woods by yourself?" Tyler asked. "I thought we were a team."

Dylan's face turned a deep red. He shuffled his feet. "I was planting evidence."

"Planting evidence? I don't get it," Kacie said.

Dylan wouldn't look at us. "I made the whole thing up. Eddy isn't my cousin. Nobody disappeared in the woods here. Before we would go searching for clues, I snuck into the woods and hid stuff for us to find."

It suddenly all made sense. We'd never found a clue when Dylan wasn't with us, and he'd never wanted us to talk to the counselors about what we'd found. I couldn't believe it. "You lied to us? We could have gotten kicked out of camp for a story you made up? I stood up for you!"

Tyler put a hand on my shoulder.

"I'm sorry," Dylan said. "It's just that I'm so short and everyone teases me. I thought if I made up this mystery, then you would be my friends."

"We would have been friends with you without the Eddy mystery. You're pretty cool," Tyler said.

A smile erased some of the misery on Dylan's face. "Forgive me?"

While the others hugged him and fussed over him, I crossed my arms. I didn't know if I could forgive him. I understood he was being teased, but I was tired of being betrayed by people who I thought were friends.

Dylan stepped over to me. "Abby? I really am sorry."

He looked so miserable that I softened and gave him a hug.

"I should get going. The director is waiting for me in his office. My parents will be here soon." Dylan gave us a sad smile. "See you guys." He headed for the office.

"People are so mean," Kacie said. She had tears in her eyes.

"Yes, they are," I said, and couldn't help but look at Noah.

His eyes met mine and then darted away.

"I guess the Eddy mystery has been solved," Tyler said.

"I'm glad we won't be going back in the woods," I said. "Now we won't have to worry about getting caught."

Kacie nodded. "Me too. Think Dylan will be okay?"

Noah was assuring her that Dylan was just dealing with junior high drama, and he'd be fine, when I tuned out their conversation.

I knew all about junior high drama. Drama happened every day in junior high. I wished I could just move on from the drama in my life, but that meant forgiving Noah. Dylan had gotten a punishment, but forgiving Noah meant he got off scot free. Besides, unforgiveness wasn't hurting me. I wasn't turning into a bitter person. I had friends, well, one friend and she was in Italy right now. Still, that meant I was doing just fine. Noah didn't deserve my forgiveness, not ever.

CHEATERS NEVER PROSPER

I LEFT MY EYES closed as I woke from a deep sleep. My thoughts drifted to Kacie and Noah. I needed to break them up, but didn't know how to without doing something cruel and without breaking my pact with Kacie. Technically, if I didn't steal Noah from her, I would be in the clear, and I wasn't stealing him, just keeping them apart. It's not like they would stay friends after camp anyway, so what was the big deal?

I stretched, opened my eyes, and screamed bloody murder. A beady-eyed, green grasshopper rested on my nose. I swiped the creepy thing off, sat up, and screamed again. I put a hand over my heart. Its rapid thumps showed me just how scared I had been.

My screams woke the other girls and they began screaming too. Grasshoppers were everywhere! On beds, in shoes, in suitcases, hopping and flying around. Esther tried to calm everyone down.

I screwed up my eyes as I watched the pandemonium below me. Noah! I swatted at a flying grasshopper, my annoyance now in control over my fear of the disgusting bugs. This was payback for the alarm clocks.

It took all of us several minutes to get rid of most of the grasshoppers and then get calmed down. Esther said if we left the door propped open, the remaining few grasshoppers would find their way out. Every one of us took a shower before breakfast. Who knew what creepy grasshopper grossness was on us? Yuck!

Kacie had to go through her entire beauty regimen (hair and makeup) before we could go to breakfast. I just pulled my wet stringy hair into a ponytail. After Kacie was told she was holding everyone up, she finally put her brush down, and we left.

I shuddered again, thinking of that grasshopper on my nose.

Kacie read my mind. "That was so gross, wasn't it? Kind of reminds me of the pond scum."

"Probably because the same person did it," I told her. "Noah."

Kacie shoved me playfully. "He did not. Why would he want to scare us like that?"

There had been no "us" about it. Noah had really been trying to scare *me*. He knew how much I hated grasshoppers. While we were walking his dog Jamie one day, a grasshopper had flown in our path startling me. I had screamed and grabbed his arm. Noah had laughed hysterically. Grasshoppers were the one bug I couldn't stand. Well, centipedes too, but I don't know anybody who likes those. "He's a jerk. I've been trying to tell you."

"He is not." Kacie stared down the path. "I don't know why you dislike him so much."

"Probably because of stinkbugs, pond muck, and grasshoppers." And for other reasons. "I'm glad you're happy he asked you to the dance, but I really think you should consider someone else."

Kacie frowned. "Like who? I don't know any other guy like I know Noah."

"It doesn't matter who. At least you'd have a chance of going with someone who might actually be a nice guy." I put my arm around her. "I just care about you." I ignored the voice in my head screaming "betrayal."

Kacie ducked from under my arm. "That's sweet, but Noah's a nice guy. Everything will be fine. You'll see." She smiled at me. "I brought this cute little sundress. I can't wait to wear it. I just know Noah will love it."

Let me guess. It was pink. "I didn't think anybody was wearing anything that dressed up. From what I heard, everyone was wearing just regular shorts and tee shirts. I know I am."

"You didn't bring a skirt or anything?" Kacie asked. "It said right in the brochure that there would be a dance."

In my mind, I could see the denim skirt I had tucked in the bottom of my suitcase. Maybe I'd find some way to wear it after I had convinced Kacie to leave her dress in her suitcase. "I didn't really read the brochure cover to cover."

Kacie blushed, like I knew she would. "Oh." She was quiet for a moment and then said, "Well, I don't think anyone will care if I wear my sundress. It's super cute."

I sighed. Kacie was not easily swayed. I had forgotten how stubborn she was. "If you think so."

"I wonder how Dylan's doing," Kacie said randomly.

I did not want to talk about Dylan. "I'm sure he's fine."

"I still can't believe he lied to us." Her voice softened. "I understand why, though." Kacie looked at me with those puppy dog brown eyes. "My mom always says nothing good comes from lying."

I averted my eyes.

"I feel guilty about being in the woods," Kacie said.

I did too, but I didn't want Kacie to start sharing all her feelings with me. Not when I was trying to break up her and Noah. I was relieved when I spotted Tyler's tall form right in front of the door. "Think Tyler's waiting on us?"

Kacie cast me a sly look. "You, maybe."

As we approached, Tyler bounded over. "We have to vote today. Finish our art projects, or go canoeing." Tyler pressed the palms of his hands together. "Please pick canoeing!"

"I don't know. I think your turtle needs some TLC," I said. "And Kacie's bowl is really good. She should finish it."

"Kacie can finish her bowl during free time," Tyler said. "Please, please, please."

Kacie giggled. "Okay. We'll vote for canoeing. I like to canoe, anyway."

"Yes!" Tyler raised his hand in the air for high-fives, and Kacie and I had to jump a little to slap his hand.

I glared at Noah immediately upon seeing him inside the dining hall. "I know you did it."

"Did what?" Noah asked, putting on a bland face.

Tyler stroked his chin. "That reminds me. How was your morning?"

"It was awful!" Kacie said right away. "Someone put grasshoppers in our cabin!"

I pointed my finger at the boys. "That someone was you two."

Tyler grinned. "I'm impressed you thought Noah and I could pull that off on our own. We got Chad to help. He wanted to after the alarm clock prank."

Kacie was speechless.

"You have to admit my prank was good," I said.

Noah laughed. "You're just lucky Chad thought it was genius or you would have been in big trouble."

Kacie looked at me. "You set their alarms?" Kacie looked at the boys. "You guys put the grasshoppers in our cabin?"

I frowned. "Don't forget the pond scum and the stinkbugs."

Tyler and Noah high fived.

I couldn't help but feel smug. "Told you," I said to Kacie.

Kacie was quiet after that.

After breakfast, our group strolled down to the pond where silver canoes were tied and waiting.

"It seems weird to be down here even though I know Eddy's disappearance was made up," Kacie said.

She was right. I took in the weeds and the soggy bank and could imagine it being the scene in a mystery novel.

"Hey!"

I turned to see Tyler and Noah joining us.

Tyler gave me a quick hug when they reached us. "Thanks for picking canoeing, ladies! This will be so much fun!" He danced a little jig that had us all giggling. "So who are partners?"

That was a silly question. I knew who Kacie and Noah would pick. Each other. But to my surprise, no one said anything. I glanced around at everyone's faces and all three were looking at the ground as if they wanted to be picked, not pick themselves.

Apparently, I was going to have to decide. The first name that popped into my head was Noah's. I studied him as my heart fluttered and my palms got sweaty. Would he even want to be in a canoe with me? The nervousness subsided as I thought about that answer. He wouldn't want to be with me. So I was down to Tyler and Kacie. I knew I should pick Kacie if I wanted to keep her and Noah apart, but her name wasn't the one that came out of my mouth. "How about Tyler and I go together." I bit my lip, wishing I could go back and say Noah's name.

Three pairs of eyes stared at me—two happy brown pairs, and a thoughtful-looking blue pair. I kept my gaze away from the blue pair. No need for Noah to see my pain.

Chad and Esther had joined everyone at the pond by now and Chad was instructing everyone to pick a partner.

Tyler slung his arm around me. "We're ahead of the game."

I rolled my eyes. He was always so corny.

Esther asked if anyone needed instructions on how to canoe, and when no hands were raised, she handed out life jackets. Then she and Chad shooed us to the canoes. Pair after pair crawled into them, trying not to tip them over.

"Do you want the front or the back?" Tyler asked. "Back does steering, front does all the work."

I tried not to giggle at his life jacket. It was way too short for him. They must not have had one his size. "Front." I tugged my life jacket down a bit. Now I was self-conscious about mine being too short. "I don't want to get blamed for running us into anything."

Tyler grinned. "I'll probably blame you anyway."

I smacked him on the shoulder. "You would."

"You guys are up," Esther called cheerfully. She held the boat while I climbed in front, Tyler in the back. Esther gave us a quick shove with her foot. "Have fun!"

"Let's catch up with Noah and Kacie," Tyler said. "Don't forget to paddle on both sides."

"Don't be a backseat driver." I paddled on one side and then the other.

Tyler cackled at my humor as he steered us in the right direction. Soon we had caught up with the other two.

"Let's have a race," Tyler said. "Losers have to serve the winners their dinner."

"Does everything have to be a competition?" I rested my paddle across my lap.

"Yes," Tyler and Noah said.

"Let's just paddle around," Kacie said, wiping water off her knee.

"Please," Tyler begged.

I could just barely see Tyler as I twisted slightly on my seat. His lower lip stuck out, so I gave in. "Fine."

Noah pointed to the other side of the pond, a good distance away. "First one to touch the bank wins."

Tyler held up his hand. "Wait. Does one person have to touch, or both?"

"Both," Noah said.

Tyler and Noah counted to three and then we were off. I thought we were gliding along at a fast pace, but Tyler started shouting instructions like we were on a rowing team. "Left, right, left, right, left, right."

He was getting on my nerves. I tried not to pay too much attention to how far ahead or behind Noah and Kacie were, but I could hear Noah's voice coaching Kacie too. When I did look, we were nose to nose.

The bank came up quicker than I thought it would. "Hurry!" Tyler yelled.

I paddled as fast and as hard as I could. Now Noah and Kacie were just a bit ahead of us. I wanted to win, bad. Without thinking, I took my paddle and shoved their canoe with all my might.

"Hey!" I heard Noah shout. Their canoe turned just enough for Tyler and me to take the lead.

Our canoe bumped the bank, and I grabbed onto a bush so Tyler could pull our canoe to the side. He touched the bank, and over my shoulder, I could see him raise his paddle in the air.

"Woohoo!" Tyler yelled.

Noah and Kacie paddled over.

"Abby cheated!" Noah said.

Kacie looked at me with wounded eyes. "You pushed us."

I had never cheated in my whole life, and I wasn't so sure I liked that I'd done it now.

"All's fair in love and war," Tyler quoted proudly. "Sorry."

I wanted to hug Tyler for sticking up for me, but I didn't want to move in the canoe and tip us into the water.

"We'll enjoy being served tonight." Tyler said. I couldn't see him, but I could imagine him pumping his fist in the air.

We paddled slowly back, which I appreciated since my muscles were burning. That was a workout!

"I can't believe you did that," Kacie whispered to me after we had banked our canoes.

I pulled at the latch on my safety jacket. "Sorry."

"I don't think you are," Kacie said. She stared at me like I was the villain in a movie.

I struggled out of my jacket, wishing someone would find a way to make them more comfortable. "Well, I did what we needed to win."

"Cheating is never winning." Kacie walked away with her chin up in the air.

I shook my head. She needed to get over herself. I wanted to call after her that sore losers weren't any better, but I kept my mouth shut.

I was disappointed in myself. I wasn't a cheater, but when I thought about Noah and Kacie having to serve me and Tyler, I was over it. It was about time something had gone my way.

LIES, LIES, AND MORE LIES

Today was the day I was going to convince Kacie that Noah was a jerk of the highest degree. Since canoeing yesterday, Kacie had been a little stand-offish. Only a small part of me had thought about how my actions would affect our friendship, if you could even call it that. I had been a reluctant friend from the beginning, a bit of a fake. Kacie truly was a frenemy.

I felt a small twinge of guilt at what I was about to do but pinched it off. Tyler was right. All was fair in love and war. If I was going to break them up, this needed to be done and fast. I kept telling myself to think about how Noah would feel when the girl he wanted was just out of reach. Maybe he'd think twice before betraying a friend.

Esther told me Kacie was in the arts and crafts building finishing her project. I found her painting her bowl a pale pink with the shell designs a soft orange. It was really pretty.

She looked up as my shadow fell over her. "Oh hey, Abby." She went back to painting, brushing slow, even strokes onto the bowl.

I shifted my feet, not having to act nervous. "I just saw something and overheard a conversation I don't think I should have."

"Was it about a murder?" Kacie dropped her brush, her eyes wide.

Trust Kacie to be so dramatic. "No, but it is bad."

"What then?" Kacie asked, sounding impatient. She flicked a strand of curly hair off her face.

"It might hurt you if I share it," I said, trying to sound like a concerned friend. I must have succeeded because Kacie's forehead wrinkled.

"If you think I should know, then you should just say it," Kacie said, after a long pause.

Here was the crossroad. The second I said my next words, I wouldn't be able to take them back. I plunged ahead. "I just saw Noah flirting with this other girl by the rec hall. She was really pretty," I added for good measure. "When I got close enough to hear what they were saying, Noah was asking her about the dance."

Kacie kept on painting. "You were spying on Noah?"

"No. I saw him flirting with this girl, like how he flirts with you, and I was concerned." I congratulated myself on my great answer. "I've been trying to tell you he's a snake."

"He was flirting with her?" Kacie's brushstrokes weren't quite so even any more.

I tried not to smile. She was worried, just like I knew she would be. "Yeah. I don't know what her name is, but I've seen Noah talking to her before."

"Do you think he asked her to go to the dance with him too?" Kacie's voice quivered.

I did my best to ignore that quiver and focused on how she'd taken the bait. "Maybe. I don't know. I didn't stick around to hear."

Kacie didn't say anything, just bit her lip, while I stood there awkwardly.

"Why aren't you two hanging out anyway? I thought you said you were going to ask him," I said. "That's why we weren't spending free time together in the first place."

Kacie was biting her lip so hard now that it was turning white. "I did ask. He said he needed to talk to someone."

I caught another smile before it could escape. Unknowingly, Noah had played right into my story. "I'm sorry." I hoped I sounded apologetic.

Kacie drew in a deep breath. "I don't know if I believe you. Maybe you just misunderstood."

"I just felt like I should tell you what I saw. I don't want you to get hurt." I waited for her to say something, but she didn't. "Well, I'm going to meet Tyler and play some ping-pong before free time is over. See you later." I left, letting the screen door slam behind me.

As soon as my feet hit the dirt path, I grinned. Victory was mine! Sure, Kacie had said maybe I had misunderstood, but her silence spoke volumes. She had just enough doubt to think maybe I was right. Good-bye, Noah and Kacie.

"What are you so happy about?" Tyler asked, practically pushing me right off the path.

I pushed him back. "Oh, I was just admiring Kacie's project," I said.

"And you're that happy?"

I could hear the doubt in his voice and I frantically tried to come up with a logical explanation. "It's really good."

Tyler let that go, much to my relief. "Weren't we supposed to play some ping-pong?"

I nodded. "That's where I was headed."

We fell into step together.

"I thought maybe you chickened out," Tyler said, tapping my shoulder.

"When have I ever chickened out?"

"Good point." He paused. "By the way, Noah was looking for you earlier."

"Noah?" Suddenly Kacie's words popped in my head. *Noah said he needed to talk to someone.* Weird. I shook my head to clear it. Tyler must be confused. Noah wouldn't want to talk to me.

After a couple of intense ping-pong matches, in which Tyler beat me soundly, I forgot all about Noah.

I didn't see Kacie again until dinner. As soon as I plopped down in my usual seat, she leaned over and whispered, "I know it was hard for you to tell me what you heard, but thanks for being honest with me."

"You're welcome. I was just trying to be a good friend."

She smiled. "I talked to Noah, and he didn't act like anything was wrong."

Words burst from my mouth. "Of course he wouldn't. He's taking two girls to the dance and thinks he's getting away with it!"

Kacie's eyes widened. Maybe I'd been a little too emotional there.

"I thought you said you weren't sure if he asked her," Kacie said, her voice still hushed.

"No. Yes. I mean it's a hunch I have," I said.

"Well, you're wrong," she whispered fiercely. Daggers shot from her eyes.

"What are you two ladies whispering about?" Tyler asked; his dark eyebrows raised.

I smiled sweetly. "Just dance stuff. Makeup, hair, you know."

Tyler nodded, stroking his chin with his index finger and thumb. "Yes. Noah and I were just discussing the same thing."

Kacie giggled. Tyler was great at diffusing tense situations, even if he didn't know why they were tense.

"I bet." I studied his tan face. "What lip gloss color did you decide on? Perfectly Pink or Cherry Red?"

"With my skin tone? Obviously, Cherry Red." Tyler fluttered his lashes.

Noah shot him a disgusted look and elbowed him.

"What? I have a fashion diva for an older sister," Tyler said.

Kacie and I were in tears from laughing so hard.

When our laughter died down, Kacie leaned toward me again. "I know you don't like Noah. Can we just let this go?"

I sighed and nodded. If I was ever going to break her and Noah up, I couldn't be fighting with her. Noah sure had a loyal friend in Kacie. I grimaced. Loyalty was not a word I wanted to think about right now.

After dinner, Noah surprised me by grabbing my arm. "I need to talk to you," he said, holding me in place as campers weaved around us.

"Your girlfriend's getting away," I said, my voice oozing with sarcasm.

Noah glared at me. "Kacie's not my girlfriend, okay? Can we please talk?"

I wrenched my arm away and crossed my arms in front of me. "About what?"

"About the dance." A hopeful look appeared on Noah's face. He gave me a tentative smile and that super cute dimple popped out.

"I don't see what we have to talk about. Not the dance because that's decided already. Kacie is obviously in love with you, so you clearly, don't need my help with that," I said. I clasped my hands to keep them from shaking.

Noah's smile disappeared along with his dimple. "That's exactly what I need help with."

Now, I was confused. "Noah, you got your girl. Besides, if you needed help, I'm the last person you should ask."

By now we were the only two left in the room, except for the staff clanking dishes and chattering.

Noah stared straight into my eyes. "You're exactly who I need."

My knees felt weak. I always melted when he looked at me that way. The way he used to before Molly.

A huge crash broke the spell and I jumped.

"I have to go. I need to catch up with the group." I ran out of the hall, ignoring Noah's call to come back.

Tears threatened as I kept running to the cabin. Every time my feet hit the ground, I repeated to myself, "I will not cry. I will not cry."

It only partially worked.

The next day, I did my best to avoid standing or sitting next to Noah and especially being alone with him. I had to admit a little part of me was curious as to what he wanted to say to me, another part of me was absolutely terrified. It couldn't be good.

That night, Kacie left me to sit with Noah at the campfire. I found an empty bench close to our group and sat down. I didn't even care if I ended up sitting by myself.

"Is this seat taken? I brought candy."

I smiled as Tyler sat down. "Maybe I was saving this seat for someone."

"You were. For me." He pulled a plastic baggie out of his sweatshirt pocket. "Hold out your hand," he instructed.

I did, and he dumped a few pieces of hard candy in my hand. I popped them in my mouth and couldn't keep my face from puckering. "Sour! Sour!" I struggled to say around the pieces. It came out sounding like "Thour! Thour!"

Tyler laughed out loud. "Your face is hilarious."

I smacked him lightly on the arm. Lucky for me, the candy had a sweet inside so the sour flavor didn't last long.

Tyler elbowed me. "Good, huh?"

I held my hand out for more, and he chuckled.

Campfire started with us singing the camp song. I swear I could hear Kacie belting it out even though she sat with Noah several rows in front of us.

We started on the next song, when I noticed the director's wife making her way down the wood plank stairs. She stopped by Kacie's seat and knelt down to talk with her.

I tapped Tyler's arm and pointed. He shrugged and kept on singing. Boys. I watched as Kacie, looking upset, followed the director's wife back up the stairs, Noah close behind.

What was going on? I got Esther's attention and asked her if I could make sure Kacie was okay. With all the singing, I wasn't sure she heard me, but she nodded. I went up the stairs and up the path but didn't see anybody. They must have been sprinting to have disappeared so quickly. Where could they have gone? That's when I heard muffled voices.

I peeked around the corner of the closest building. I must have misunderstood the expression on Kacie's face because she sure didn't look upset now.

Noah's hands rested on Kacie's waist and hers were on his shoulders. Kacie looked up at Noah with adoration. My imagination went wild. Noah was going to kiss

Kacie! Before I even knew what I was doing, I marched right over to them and tapped Noah on the shoulder.

He jumped, paling when he saw me standing there. He dropped his hands from Kacie's waist and backed away from her.

"What are you doing?" I yelled at him as loud as I could. "Could you be any more of a jerk?"

"What's going on, Abby?" Kacie asked, her eyes wide.

I stood, facing Noah. "What's going on is that a few months ago, I thought Noah was my boyfriend, but then he took my biggest enemy to the Winter Dance, and now he's kissing you right in front of me."

"Kissing?" Noah shook his head. "I wasn't kissing Kacie."

I put my hands on my hips and snickered. "Right. I know what I saw."

Noah glared at me. "You don't know anything, Abby. Kacie's dad called. Her grandma's really sick, and he's picking Kacie up early from camp. Since she's going to miss the dance, I told her we could have a dance right now."

I deflated quickly. Embarrassment swept over me, and I could feel my cheeks flaming. "Oh"—I turned to Kacie—"I'm so sorry, Kacie. I didn't know." I moved toward her so I could give her a hug, but she backed away.

"You and Noah were boyfriend-girlfriend?" Kacie had a strange light in her eye. "You knew Noah this whole time and didn't tell me?"

I stumbled my way through an explanation feeling defensive. "Well, we made that pact and then you saw

Noah and I tried to tell you, but you kept interrupting me. Then I just didn't want to say anything."

Kacie gasped. "You tried to sabotage my relationship with Noah!" She pointed her finger at me. "You told me he asked someone else to the dance! You told me he was a big jerk! None of that was true, was it? You were just jealous!"

"Kacie—"

"You should be ashamed of yourself, Abby. And using Tyler too. You're the jerk!" Kacie shouted.

"No! I'm not a jerk! And I didn't use Tyler!" I yelled back.

Sparks leapt from her eyes. "Oh, yes, you did. You were using Tyler to make Noah jealous!"

"What? No! Tyler and I are just friends," I protested. "I would never do that."

Kacie laughed, but it wasn't a happy sound. "I don't believe you." Then she turned on Noah. "You lied to me too."

"I never lied to you, Kacie. I just didn't think my past with Abby mattered," Noah said.

I flinched. It didn't matter?

"You didn't think your past with my camp best friend mattered?" Kacie said. She pushed Noah in the chest.

I flinched again. I had never really thought of Kacie as a friend.

"I'm sorry, Kacie. I just didn't think," Noah replied, reaching to grab her hand.

Tears filled Kacie's eyes and she yanked her hand back. "I don't ever want to see you guys again." She ran away and neither Noah nor I tried to follow.

I should have been happy. Elated even. I had just accomplished exactly what I wanted to. Kacie had dumped Noah. Instead of feeling better that I had gotten my revenge, I felt worse. I had hurt Kacie, and, by the looks of things, she was far more heartbroken than Noah.

When I looked at Noah, he was glaring at me. "Way to go, Abby." He stomped off.

I stood alone wondering how I could fix the colossal mess I had created. I hung out there for a while, thinking about Esther's devotion on forgiveness. Now, I realized I should have listened. Wanting revenge *had* hurt me. I'd lied, cheated, been jealous and fake. I wished I could rewind and start over, but I'd made my choice. As I stood there wondering what I should do, I saw Esther approaching.

"What are you doing out here all by yourself?"

"Thinking." For the first time in a long time, that answer was actually the truth. It felt good.

"The woods are a great place to do that. I love to star gaze and think. Pray." Esther raised her head and looked at the stars.

I glanced up at the sky too, and it took my breath away. Millions of stars twinkled in the blackness. It was absolutely beautiful. "How have I missed this?"

"Sometimes, we forget to look up," Esther said, gazing at the stars. "So what are you thinking about?"

I decided to tell her the whole story. It was nice to get it all out there with someone who wasn't involved. Even though it didn't change anything, I felt like a hundred pound weight had just been lifted off my shoulders. I hadn't even known I was carrying it.

"Wow," Esther said softly when I had finished. She paused. "You know, there's a verse in the Bible where God says vengeance is His. There's a reason we're not supposed to take that on."

"But didn't Noah deserve to be punished? He hurt me!"

Esther pushed her hair behind her ears. "I know he did. But now you've hurt someone too. Kacie. And she didn't do anything wrong, except to get caught in the middle of you and Noah."

I let my head flop forward. Instead of anger and hurt, I felt shame. Lots of it.

Esther lifted my chin with her index finger. "Do you deserve to be punished for that?"

My *yes* was almost inaudible.

"God is merciful to his children. Sometimes, I don't think that seems fair either, but when I think of all the times I've hurt people, I'm very grateful for that mercy," Esther said. She dropped her hand from my chin and looked back up at the stars. "When people hurt you, you can pour out all that hurt to God, forgive them as many times as that pain resurfaces, and trust him to take care of the rest." She put her arm around me. "Believe me when I say I know it's not easy, but it is the right choice to make. Unforgiveness is like a cancer that eats away at our soul."

Oh, how I knew that was true. The last few weeks, all I'd been focused on was revenge, and I hadn't cared what lies I'd told or who I'd hurt. "So what do I do now?"

Esther smiled. "What do you think?"

"Apologize and hope they forgive me." I didn't deserve Kacie or Noah's forgiveness, but I sure hoped for it, maybe the same way Noah had hoped for mine.

"Absolutely. And remember, even if they don't forgive you, God has. You're still pretty cool in his book." Esther hugged me. "And in mine."

A peace I hadn't felt in a very long time settled on me. I wished I would have talked with Esther about this way earlier. "I'll go talk to Kacie right now."

Esther yawned widely. "I'm going to bet Kacie is asleep. We've been out here a long time."

"The campfire is over?" I asked, shocked.

"Long over." She began walking toward the cabin, and I followed. "The director's wife was keeping an eye on you. She sent me out here to talk to you thinking you might need a friend."

As we entered the sleeping cabin, I was torn by relief and disappointment that I couldn't talk to Kacie until the morning. I just wanted to get it over and done with, but I was afraid of what she would say. Kacie might forgive me, but would Noah?

APOLOGY ACCEPTED?

I DIDN'T SLEEP WELL, so when I heard Kacie rustling around, I sat up quickly, almost bonking my head on the ceiling. "Kacie," I whispered loudly. I hung my head over the bed.

She was rolling up her pink sleeping bag, clearly ignoring me. I clambered down the bunk bed steps. "Can I talk to you?"

Kacie kept her back to me. She wound the strings around her bag and tied them.

Even though she hadn't acknowledged me, I started in on my apology before I chickened out. "I'm so sorry about everything. I was an awful friend to you. I'm sorry for lying to you and for trying to sabotage you and Noah. It was wrong. Please forgive me."

Kacie didn't say a word. Instead, she picked up her suitcase and set it on her bed. She opened it and placed her neatly folded pink pajamas inside.

"Kacie?"

"Well, you got what you wanted," she finally said, still keeping her back to me. "I'm not going to the dance with Noah, so he's all yours."

Noah wouldn't have wanted to go to the dance with me before, and now he definitely wouldn't. "No," I told her firmly. "We made a pact." I clutched the cold metal bed post with a white knuckled grip.

Kacie snorted. "Like that ever mattered to you."

I rested my head against the post. "I won't lie and say I was never jealous, but I never meant to hurt you. Promise."

Kacie shook her head. "I feel so stupid. The whole time, you and Noah lying to me."

"I'm sorry." I didn't know what else to say. I had really messed things up with her.

She looked up at me and I was taken aback by the coldness in her usually warm brown eyes. "No one has ever treated me the way you have, so I'm not going to pretend we're okay."

Tears pricked my eyes. Sweet, loveable Kacie was not going to forgive me.

She refolded a shirt. Her suitcase was neat and organized. "But I will forgive you," she said.

"Really?" My voice sounded squeaky, so I cleared my throat and repeated, "Really?" I felt relieved. Those were not words I'd expected to hear at all.

Kacie stuffed her creek stomping shoes into a separate compartment of her suitcase. They were no longer sparkling white, but mud-colored. "Really."

I wanted to hug her, but judging from the stiff and tense way she was carrying herself, I decided not to push it. "Thank you."

She zipped her pink and white polka dotted suitcase shut and set it on the ground carefully so as not to wake any of the other campers. Kacie was always thinking of others. "I have to go."

I nodded. "I hope your grandma gets better."

Kacie rubbed her eyes. I couldn't tell if she was crying or just tired. Maybe both. "Thanks." She wheeled her suitcase around, and I held the screen door open for her. Before she carried her suitcase down the cabin steps, Kacie paused. "Please tell Noah and Tyler I said good-bye."

"I will," I said. If they were still speaking to me. I watched with an ache in my heart as she disappeared down the path.

My time with Kacie was done. For so much of it, I had been fake and downright mean, and I regretted it. For all the times her chirpiness annoyed me, Kacie was a much better person than I. If I had given her a chance, I bet we could have become good friends. Maybe we would even have e-mailed each other after camp was over.

I imagined the conversation Kacie would have with her parents about her time at camp. Would she tell them about all the awful things I'd done? If it were me, I would at least tell Claire about the jerk girl who had pretended to be my friend. Claire would be outraged as I told her how this girl had tried to break me and Noah up. Shame washed over me. I deserved every mean thing Kacie said about me.

Feeling dejected, I went back in the cabin and climbed back in bed, trying to be quiet so I didn't wake anybody up. There was no reason to rush to breakfast. I wasn't sure there would be anyone there willing to talk to me.

I sat on the other side of the table at breakfast since I was pretty sure neither Noah nor Tyler would want to see me. The table seemed quiet without Kacie's chatter, even though the other girls were talking and giggling. Before the boys left the dining hall, I tried to catch Noah's attention so I could apologize, but he ignored me. Even Tyler acted like he hadn't seen me. Did he feel used, like Kacie had suggested last night? I hoped not, because I had never used Tyler. I genuinely liked him. As much as I had wanted Noah to ask me to the dance, I had been okay about going with Tyler. He was always so much fun.

After breakfast, we were supposed to go back to the cabin to clean up our space and pack everything but what we would need for tonight and tomorrow. Once we were done, we were free until the dance. Kacie had been very neat and tidy, so I didn't have much to do, other than pick up my clothes that had ended up under the bed due to my messiness. I asked Esther if it was okay to spend my free time in the arts and crafts building. It would be quiet there, and I could finish my art project. When she agreed, I was relieved. I needed the privacy.

My bowl didn't look anything like Kacie's. It was lopsided, definitely wouldn't be able to hold anything, and the design I'd picked, a swirly pattern, was smeared, but I was still semi-proud of it. I picked up a paint brush and dipped it into the forest green paint. If I put it in front of a fan, it should dry in time to take home, but there wouldn't be time to fire it again to make the paint look shiny. I tried to be as careful as Kacie had been, but I still ended up with paint streaks on my hands and arms. The quiet and the peace soothed me.

Before I knew it, it was time to get ready for the dance. I set my bowl on newspaper to dry and headed back to the cabin. Quietly I changed into my jean skirt and my favorite dressy purple shirt. It always made me feel so grown-up. The other girls primped and giggled, excited about the evening. I slumped down on Kacie's bed with my head in my hands wondering what her sundress looked like. She'd never shown it to me.

I followed the other girls down to the rec hall and immediately went to find the punch while they ooh'd and aah'd over the decorations. Candles were on every table, flickering light on the walls. Purple and green streamers hung from the ceiling. A sparkly disco ball hung over the middle of the dance floor. The food table was heaped with all kinds of scrumptious goodies.

It was the kind of atmosphere that made everyone believe in fairy tales, except me. I didn't anticipate this night to be any fun at all. I hadn't talked to Tyler all day, and he hadn't tried to find me either, so I guessed our date was off. The most excitement for me would be trying to decide if I should pick a frosted brownie or an unfrosted one. I couldn't be too upset, though. I had done this to myself.

The other girls from my cabin had formed a little group on one side of the room. I decided not to join them, and after refilling my cup of red punch, picked a metal folding chair in the corner. More campers came in, but I paid little attention, content to sip my punch. After I had drunk it all, I got up, threw my cup away, and decided to get some fresh air.

As I opened the door, there stood Noah and Tyler. Noah looked so cute in his plaid shorts and polo shirt. My heart hung in my throat. Before my opportunity was wasted, I let the door shut, and said, "I'm sorry, Noah."

Tyler slipped around us and went inside. I didn't take my eyes off Noah.

His blue eyes should have been red with all the fire in them. "It's too late for that now, Abby. Way too late."

Tears filled my eyes. The tone in his voice sounded a lot like hatred. I deserved it. Oh, how I deserved it, but it hurt. Somehow, I knew the forgiveness Kacie had extended to me, would not be given to me by Noah. "What do you mean?"

Noah shook his head. "You still don't get it, do you?"

"Please help me understand." Tears spilled down my cheeks.

"Ugh!" Noah cried out. Frustration was written all over his face. "I asked Molly to the dance when you couldn't go, because all of her friends had dates, and she was going to have to go alone. We danced one dance together and then the rest of the time she was with her friends."

A pity date? I had caused all this drama over a pity date? "I wish I had known," I whispered, still trying to wrap my mind around the fact that he hadn't liked Molly.

Noah threw his hands up. "I tried to tell you, Abby. More than once, but you wouldn't listen."

I stared at my sparkly purple sandals.

"When I saw you here and then we ended up in the same group, I thought, great, maybe we can start over. I'll be able to make things right," Noah said.

"We can still have a second chance! I want to start over." I sniffled, wishing I had a tissue.

Noah looked me straight in the eye. "I don't want to any more. Not after all of this. I don't care that you were trying to get back at me, but to hurt Kacie too? That's not cool, Abby. Not cool at all. I don't want to hang out with a person like that." He took a step forward to go inside.

I grabbed his arm, desperate to keep him from leaving. "Please don't go, Noah."

"Don't touch me." He jerked his arm away.

As soon as he disappeared into the rec hall, I ran to the back side of the building, leaned against the wall, and slid to a sitting position. All of the emotions I'd stuffed inside for the past couple of weeks came hurtling out in one big sob fest. I was a mess.

After my tears were spent, I hefted myself up and trudged back to my cabin. I had no desire to go back to the dance at all and didn't care if I got in trouble for being there by myself. Camp was over tomorrow anyway. As I approached the cabin, I saw a dark figure sitting on the steps. Tyler? What was he doing here? I hoped he hadn't come to ream me out too.

I sat down next to him, feeling cautious. "How's the dance?"

Tyler shrugged. "Boring. The girls are standing on one side, the boys on the other. But that's not the worst thing."

"What?" I asked out of politeness. I wasn't sure I wanted to know what the worst thing was.

"My date stood me up." He hung his head.

I tried not to giggle from relief. Tyler wasn't mad at me. "Sorry," I said, wiping my nose on my sleeve. "I didn't think you still wanted to hang out with me. No one else does."

Tyler put his arm around me. "So you screwed up. Friends don't bail on each other."

I leaned my head against his shoulder. "Thanks."

We sat like that for a while, listening to the crickets, the rustle of leaves, and the faint sound of music playing.

Tyler lifted his arm from my shoulders and grabbed a familiar plastic bag out of his pocket. "Candy?" He held the bag open.

I smiled, reached in the bag, and then popped a few pieces in my mouth. Tyler was my hero.

Tyler stood up and offered me his hand. "Come on. It's the last night. Let's make it a night to remember."

I hesitated before taking his hand. "Yeah, why not. Who knows when we'll see each other again."

"Exactly. Let's go skip rocks on the pond." He pulled me up.

I brushed the dirt off my skirt. "I don't know how to do that. Besides, it's dark."

Tyler grinned and arched an eyebrow. "Chicken?" He started down the path to the pond, knowing I would follow. "I'll have you know I was the champion rock-skipper at my school. Fifteen skips. It's the record."

I laughed. "You'll have to prove it."

"Oh, I will." He started running. "Last one there has to eat a lightening bug."

"Gross!" I shouted. I chased after him. There was no way I was going to catch those long legs of his, and I'd rather die than eat a lightening bug. "Tyler! Wait! I think I sprained my ankle!"

I heard him come back as I kneeled down on the path.

"Are you okay? Did you trip?" Tyler crouched next to me.

I popped up. "Gotcha! Hope you like lightening bugs!"

"Cheater!" I heard Tyler yell. I could also hear his laughter.

At least I hadn't screwed this up. I could learn a thing or two about friendship from Tyler. One thing I knew for sure, I was never ever going to be the person I'd been these last two weeks again. I had learned my lesson. Maybe someday, Noah and I could put all this drama behind us, and be friends again. Maybe someday.